WRATH
APHRODITE

BESS T. CHAPPAS

outskirtspress

DENVER, COLORADO

Outskirts Press, Inc.
http://www.outskirtspress.com

ISBN: 978-1-4787-4643-0

Outskirts Press and the "OP" logo are trademarks belonging to Outskirts Press, Inc.

This book is dedicated to the indisputably beautiful and unique city of Savannah and to the people who make Savannah their home, especially to those who remember life in the 1970s.

Other books by Bess Chappas:

Kiki and the Red Shoes

Kiki and the Statue of Liberty

Acknowledgements

Many thanks to the members of the Tuesday Writers Group of Senior Citizens, Inc. of Savannah, for their thoughtful critique and excellent suggestions during the writing of this novel. To Betty Darby for her meticulous editing, and to Larry Teuton for sharing his knowledge of boats and Savannah area waterways. If errors slipped through, the fault is mine. Additional thanks for my grandson and tech guru, Christopher Teuton.

Pinkie Masters was a well known, and well loved, Savannah personality. Although he died in 1977, the bar is still a favorite hangout for locals and tourist. Other than the use of his name and place of business, Masters' actions in the story are figments of my imagination. I knew Pinkie and his family personally, therefore I don't believe he would mind my using him as a pivotal character.

Some readers will recognize places in Savannah as they existed in the 1970s. If my geography or time-line is a little off, remember this is fiction. The New Smyrna Colony established in Florida in the 1760s is an historic fact. Information about this can be obtained at the St. Photios

Shrine in St. Augustine, FL or by reading **New Smyrna, An Eighteenth Century Greek Odyssey** by E.P. Panagopoulos. There is no record of a marble statue connected with the New Smyrna Colony.

Prologue

"That damn Michael is getting too big for his britches. I can't even find him this morning," said Steve Dugan, pit boss for Crimson Lights, a Las Vegas Casino, as he entered the upstairs room with the two-way mirrors. "I know you hired the Greek because you think he's charming and has a pretty face, but I'd like for Rocco to rearrange it for him."

The TV screens in the room were manned by Big Duke Lenski, owner of the casino. He turned in his chair and gave Steve a crooked grin, showing tobacco-stained teeth. Lenski didn't earn his nickname, Big Duke, from being tall, but from his broad frame. He had shoulders like a fullback and a barrel chest. His huge muscular arms ended with fingers thick as sausages. His immense torso tapered down to short stubby legs. Steve was his brother-in-law and the only one of his men who could stand up to him when he glared at them with unblinking crocodile eyes beneath black bushy eyebrows.

"Well, Steve. You're going to get your wish 'cause the Greek is on his way out. Been suspecting something was going on with him and the McKinney brothers. When those goddamn Texans took us for all that money last night and Andrews wasn't even around, I was sure of it. I got Rocco looking for him now. When he finishes with him, Andrews will wish he never stepped foot in Vegas."

Meanwhile, Michael Andrews closed his eyes and leaned against the back of the elevator as he rode down to the casino area. Staying up all night with high-rollers was wearing him down. As a host for a Las Vegas casino, it was his job, to cater to the special guests, those who spent thousands of dollars. Whatever they wanted, he had to supply. High rollers didn't take cabs from the airport, carry their own bags, or wait in check-in lines. They stayed in rooms with Jacuzzis, circular leather couches, wide-screen TV, and had their call girls waiting for them upstairs.

He couldn't complain about the pay, but Michael was tired of having to be at the guests' beck and call. He felt like a whore, acting like their best friend while enticing them to spend more money. But the acting jobs in Hollywood had dried up and he didn't know what else to do. He doubted if his mother and father would consider his job respectable. He wished he hadn't thought about his parents since it always made him feel guilty.

Because he was sick of his job, he was taking dangerous chances, like going out last night with a woman he met at the bar, instead of staying with the Texans at the gaming tables. Andrews figured the McKinney brothers were winning big because they were using some kind of card counting system. He knew he should report it to Steve, the pit boss, but he was getting big tips from them, so he kept quiet. He supposed they would leave when they won as much as they felt was safe and no one would be the wiser.

From the lobby, Michael walked downstairs into the cafeteria going directly to the buffet for coffee and a sandwich. He noticed Lou, a casino security guard, sitting at a table across the room. Lou was a retired cop from Chicago and they had formed a kind of friendship while reminiscing about the windy city.

Michael was halfway across the cafeteria when Lou looked up and saw him coming toward him. Lou's face flushed red as he jumped up from the table, rattling dishes and spilling water. He ran to Michael and grabbed his arm.

"What the hell are you doing here? I thought you skipped town with the Texans. Rocco is looking for you and if he grabs you, it won't be pretty."

"What the devil are you talking about?" Michael's gut clenched when he saw the fear in Lou's face.

"Here, put that food down on the table and listen. The McKinneys cleaned out the blackjack table last night. The dealer became suspicious and reported to the boss, but the Texans left the casino and took off in a private plane before anyone could find them. That son-of-bitch, Lenski, thinks you knew what they were doing."

"Rocco is looking for you upstairs. You're lucky he hasn't found you yet. Man, I'm telling you—Get. Out. Now!"

Michael looked into Lou's eyes and recognized terror. "Thanks, buddy," he whispered. Then, he fled Vegas with only the suit on his back—thank God it was the Armani—and the money he had in his pocket.

Chapter 1

Michael stood on Emmett Park bluff overlooking River Street, watching a huge cargo ship slowly drift down the Savannah River toward the Atlantic Ocean. His thoughts drifted like the ship as he envisioned stowing away on the vessel and leaving his problems behind. Rubbing his red-rimmed eyes, he searched the pockets of his Armani jacket for his little silver flask of Scotch and took a few sips to calm his nerves. *Pull yourself together. You're in trouble, but there's got to be a way out of this,* Michael told himself.

Women passing by noticed the tall, well-built young man with startling blue-green eyes. His full, sensuous mouth pulled down at the corners as he ran his hand over curly black hair that almost met his collar at the back of his neck. A small scar on his chin kept his face from being Adonis perfect.

Unaware of the beauty of Savannah all around him, Michael left Emmett Park and walked the few blocks south to the DeSoto Hotel. He didn't notice the majestic live oak trees laden with Spanish moss or the many hued azaleas blooming underneath the ancient trees as he walked through the famous Savannah squares. He paid no attention to the historic houses that graced the narrow streets, some built very close together as if they needed the company. His thoughts were on the events of the last couple days and his hurried flight out of Las Vegas.

He'd arrived in Savannah, Georgia the day before to see Pinkie Masters, his godfather and his father's oldest friend. His plan was to borrow money to leave the country, maybe to visit relatives in Greece, but he didn't want to ask right away. He was ashamed to let Pinkie see how desperate and how frightened he was because of what had happened in Vegas.

Pinkie Masters Lounge on the corner of Drayton and Harris Streets was one of the city's favorite watering holes and hangout for local politicians. Even President Jimmy Carter, a personal friend of Pinkie's, stopped in whenever he came to town.

Michael entered the bar and stood just inside the door. Yes, the place looked as he remembered. The room was small and dim, with a horseshoe shaped bar and a few booths made of dark wood. An old juke box fought to be heard over the loud talk and laughter of the customers. Election posters and pictures of local and visiting dignitaries covered the dingy walls along with framed scenes of old Savannah sites. Prominently displayed behind the bar were pictures of President Jimmy Carter and Pinkie taken during Carter's presidential campaign in Georgia.

"Michael, my boy, what a surprise," said Pinkie, around

the ever present cigarette dangling out of his mouth. Coming around the bar, he shook Michael's hand and put his arm around his godson's shoulder. "Welcome to Savannah. How's Gus and the family?"

"They're doing well," Michael lied. He'd had no contact with his family for several years. "Business is good at the restaurant. My brother is married and has kids of his own. The Andropoulos family is growing."

"Good, good," replied Pinkie. "What can I get you to drink?"

"Well, it's a little early for me, but I'll have a bit of Scotch if you insist," replied Michael.

"Take a seat at the bar and I'll introduce you to the regulars."

Throughout the afternoon, Michael met many of Pinkie's customers. The bar's clientele were downtown workers who stopped in for a break, politicians who wheeled and dealed in the back booths, members of old Savannah families, and scruffy street people looking for a handout. They all greeted Pinkie by name.

With his sexy looks and expensive clothes, Michael was a magnet for women. From the time Michael was sixteen, he could have any woman he wanted. Women, old enough to be his mother, begged to teach him the fine art of lovemaking. In high school, girls considered it an honor to lose their virginity to Michael and he was always glad to oblige. Tonight, however, to the disappointment of several women customers, Michael kept his head down and his eyes on his drink before him.

Later that evening, Pinkie introduced Michael to Winston C. Boudreau, a retired Georgia state senator.

Michael was impressed with Boudreau's classic southern charm and his sophisticated bearing. He envied the power that emanated from the senator.

"Sit down, Michael, and tell me about yourself," encouraged Boudreau. "Call me Senator. Everybody does." Boudreau's sable brown eyes gleamed with interest and intelligence. A long-fingered hand with manicured nails swept back a snow white lock of hair from his high forehead.

Michael told him he had dropped out of college to try his hand at acting in Hollywood. "I managed to get a few small parts and did some modeling," he told the senator, "but the jobs stopped coming. Hollywood is a closed shop to outsiders. If you aren't related to a big star or know an important person in management, you are out of luck." He didn't tell the older man that his drinking and drug use soon gave him a bad reputation with the casting agencies.

"I decided to try someplace else and left Hollywood and moved to Las Vegas where I found work in a casino as a host," continued Michael. "My main duty was to take care of the guests and entice the high rollers to spend more money. I believe I did a good job but got tired of it." Michael didn't tell Boudreau he got over friendly with a couple of Texas players and caused the casino to lose a considerable amount of money. Neither did he say that he was afraid the owners, who had mob connections, would likely send someone after him.

The senator listened to Michael, sensing more than Michael wanted him to know. "Well, boy, I enjoyed talking with you but I better be getting along home. Say, tomorrow is Sunday. If you don't have any plans, why not drive out to the old homestead and have supper with us? I'd like to show you my new boat. You like to sail, don't you?"

"Thank you, sir. I'd like that. I did a little sailing when I was in college. And, I don't know anyone in town except for Pinkie."

"Good. Pinkie can give you directions how to get to the house." With a wave to Pinkie, Boudreau left the bar.

"Well Michael, you made a good friend there. The Senator is old Savannah and a respected man, not only locally, but the whole state of Georgia…His folks probably came over with General Oglethorpe. If you decide to stay in Savannah for a while, he can help you find a job," said Pinkie. "He has a fancy place off of Highway 17."

Maybe my luck is about to change, thought Michael. *Knowing a rich and influential man can't hurt.*

Chapter 2

The next day, Michael climbed into his rental car, and armed with directions from Pinkie, drove forty minutes on US 17 south toward the Boudreau estate. At a sign that read Magnolia Bluff, he took a right into a narrow blacktop that led to a curved driveway and a three story Greek revival mansion painted white with dark green shutters. The house had a flat roof with twin chimneys with four Doric columns supporting the front portico. Around the mansion grew stately Magnolias and behind them, tall Georgia pines.

A large, manicured garden extended to the right of the house. Michael could see a marble statue of a woman, a goddess, standing in the middle of a bed of azaleas and variegated spring flowers. On the left side of the house, a section of wooden deck was visible. *Down that way must be the sailboat the senator mentioned,* he thought.

He parked the car, stepped under the portico and pulled an ornate brass bell. A heavy-set woman wearing a black dress and a white apron opened the door. She inspected Michael with sharp ebony eyes.

"May I help you, suh?"

"I'm Michael Andrews. I believe the senator is expecting me."

"Yes suh, this way please. The senator is in the study."

Michael followed the woman through a spacious foyer floored with white and black marble tile. The walls were decorated with landscape art in heavy gold frames. The woman led him down a hall into another room where the senator sat behind a large partner's desk smoking a cigar. Soft glowing lights gave a rich sheen to the polished antique furniture. Shelves circled the walls, filled with expensive looking books. It was a man's room and it smelled of money.

"There you are, Michael," boomed Boudreau, as he rose from his leather wingback chair. "Thank you, Maggie. You can serve dinner in half an hour." Turning to the younger man, he asked, "Scotch, isn't it?"

"Yes, thank you," Michael answered. He stood until Boudreau handed him the drink and returned to his chair. Before he could sit down, a woman's voice, like molasses over whiskey, came from the doorway.

"Sorry I'm late, Daddy."

Michael turned to see a tall slim woman wearing dark slacks and a white silk blouse glide into the room on four-inch heels. Pearls circled her throat and dangled from her ears. Long dark hair floated around a face, pale as marble. Her eyes, dark and heavy lidded, captured his.

"You're not late," the senator answered. "Our guest just now got here. "Stephanie, this is Michael Andrews, Pinkie's godson and new to Savannah. Michael this is Stephanie, my daughter."

Michael took her hand and gazed into her eyes. The

pupils were like pin points. *Drugs*, he thought. Stephanie withdrew her hand and turned to her father.

"How about one of those drinks for me?" She quietly assessed Michael, his long, lean body, his handsome face, and those incredible turquoise eyes.

"Sure," said the senator, returning to the bar across the room from his desk. "You can take it into the dining room. I see Maggie hovering at the door. Dinner must be ready."

Sitting across the table from Stephanie, Michael was surprised to find that her eyes were not dark as he had first surmised; they were hazel with golden flecks around the irises. *Cat eyes. If I touch her, will she purr or will she scratch*, he wondered.

During dinner, Stephanie glanced at Michael surreptitiously, admiring his handsome physique and gorgeous eyes surrounded with dark spiky lashes. *Any woman would kill to have eyes like that*, she thought.

While they enjoyed Maggie's sumptuous dinner of roast beef, Savannah red rice, crispy salad, local vegetables, and followed with fresh peach pie, Boudreau watched the pair covertly. He could sense the hum of attraction between Stephanie and Michael as they made small talk about what to do and where to go in Savannah.

"Have you seen our River Street?" Stephanie asked Michael. "The river is becoming Savannah's number one tourist attraction. After dinner, I'm going downtown to meet some friends. Would you like to come with me?"

Before he could reply, Boudreau surprised Michael by saying, "The boy and I have some business to take care of. Maybe he'll see you down there later."

After Stephanie said her good-byes and left the dining room, Michael looked at Boudreau expectantly with a glint of annoyance in his eyes. "What's going on, Senator?"

"Now, now, boy, don't get your shorts in a wad. Let's go back to the study." He led the way across the hall and sat behind his desk. Taking a cigar from an inlaid mahogany humidor, he lit it slowly. "Would you like one?" he asked Michael. "Good stuff. Have a friend in Cuba."

Reaching for his cigarettes, Michael shook his head. "I appreciate the dinner and the hospitality, Senator, but I'd like to know what the hell is going on."

"You can cut out the act, boy. Who do you think you're fooling? I have friends in Vegas and made a call this morning so I know all about you and the trouble you're in." Michael's gut coiled in fear. When he moved to get up, the senator continued, "Sit, sit, I didn't tell anyone that you're in Savannah. Just listen, boy, I'm trying to help you."

Michael was rattled, but he was determined not to let it show. He was proud that his hands were steady as he lit his cigarette. "There're some pretty nasty people after me, even though I didn't steal any of their money. The truth is I'm planning to ask Pinkie for money to leave the country for a while. Maybe go to Greece."

"I'm sure Pinkie will help you all he can, but he doesn't have a lot of cash right now. A real estate investment went bad on him few months ago. I know because I was involved myself, but I have the resources to take the hit without getting hurt."

"If what you say is true, I'll just have to move on. I can't stay where those damn guys from Vegas can find me. I have other prospects," Michael lied.

"I don't think you do. I've checked around. You're in big trouble and have nowhere to run. However, I have a proposition for you that will solve your problems."

Michael began to squirm in his chair. He couldn't help it. Preparing to bolt, he started to put out his cigarette.

The senator placed his cigar in an ornate ashtray. Then, he leaned forward, his eyes piercing Michael's.

"This is what you can do. You can marry my daughter."

Chapter 3

M ichael was stunned. The heat of the cigarette on his finger cleared his head. Stubbing it out on a crystal ashtray, he got to his feet. "What? Are you crazy? I just met your daughter. I have enough problems without taking on a wife. I'm not that desperate."

"I don't know. I think you are. Sit back down and let's talk about this calmly." Boudreau walked to the bar and poured brandy into two snifters, giving one to Michael. "Would a million dollars make you listen to what I have to say?"

Michael downed the brandy in one gulp. Then he went to the bar, poured himself another, and sat back down. "Okay, I'm listening."

"Good," said the senator. "Hear me out. Two years ago, when Stephanie graduated from college she became engaged to a man she met at school. He was from an old influential New England family. He had finished law school and was going into his father's firm. Stephanie was crazy about the guy, but his family thought he could do better than a girl they considered from the backwater south. They convinced him to wait six months before they got married, and the next thing Stephanie knew he had gone back to his old girlfriend, who was someone his parents believed more suitable for their son. My daughter took it extremely hard." Boudreau looked away from Michael and rubbed his hand over his eyes.

"In fact Stephanie had a nervous breakdown. When she came out of the hospital, she was not the same girl. Since then, she drinks too much, fools around with drugs, hangs out with a sleazy group down on River Street, and doesn't listen to anything I say. Stephanie is my only child and I am very concerned about her."

"I know you're in trouble, Michael, but from what I found out, you come from a good, stable family. If you're finished sowing your wild oats, this could be a second chance for you as well as for Stephanie. She's a beautiful girl. I could tell that you noticed. She's smart, too, when she is not drinking. If I got you a job here in Savannah, would you stay and think about it?"

Michael's head was spinning. "I can't say I'm not interested in getting to know a beautiful girl, but what makes you think Stephanie will go for this?" He couldn't help but smile at the irony of the situation. In his experience, fathers usually warned him to stay away from their daughters. This one was throwing his daughter at him.

"Well now, that's up to you. You're a good-looking man and I don't think you're inexperienced when it comes to women. We wouldn't tell her about our arrangement, of course. I will help you find a job, and give you a million dollars as a wedding present. Will you think about it?"

Back at the DeSoto Hotel, Michael changed into jeans and t-shirt. He walked north to Bay Street, passing through squares planned and constructed by General Oglethorpe when Savannah was founded in 1733. Oblivious of the history surrounding him, Michael climbed down narrow iron steps to River Street, and headed for the closest bar. A full moon peeking in and out of dark gray clouds flickered on the street built of stones used for ship's ballast two hundred years ago, giving the narrow street a slick wet look. Michael walked into the first bar he encountered, climbed on a stool, and ordered a drink.

After a double Scotch, Michael was mellow enough to consider the senator's proposition. A million dollars! That's a lot of money. He wouldn't have to stay in Savannah forever. With that kind of money, he could go anywhere he wanted. Stephanie was a gorgeous woman. He'd slept with a lot worse, especially when he was drinking.

Then, there was the senator's property. What an inheritance that would be. He'd like to see his father's face when he found out how much Michael would be worth. He'd like to stick it to the old man. Michael remembered his father, yelling at him, his face red, when Michael told him he didn't want any part of the restaurant business and that he was leaving for Hollywood.

Chicago, IL   1969

It was seven years ago that Michael came home during his sophomore year at college and told his mother and father that he had flunked out of school and didn't intend to return.

"I don't understand," said his mother. "You always made good grades." Anna's eyes, so much like her son's, filled with tears as she looked at Michael. Still a beautiful woman at fifty, her blond hair was just beginning to streak with gray. Her fair good looks were typical of the northern part of Greece where the people were blond and blue-eyed, just like the ancient Greeks in the history books she often read to Michael when he was young.

"I'm just not interested in business; all those courses in accounting and statistics are boring. I've been taking some classes in acting at the school and everyone says I have talent. I want to go to Hollywood and get into the movies."

"What's wrong with you?" shouted his father. Why can't you be more like your brother, Deno. He finished college and is managing one of the restaurants. Why did I work so hard all my life if it wasn't for you boys? I wanted you to have a college education, but if you don't want to go to school, that's okay. You can work in one of the restaurants until you get some experience and later, you can manage it."

Gus Andropoulos came to America when he was fifteen. After a short time in New York City, he drifted to Chicago where he found a job as a dishwasher in a Greek restaurant. After several years of hard work, careful planning, and luck, he had become owner of two restaurants. Already a successful business man at thirty, he went back to Greece for a visit. With his tall strong figure and the scent of American money, he attracted the best looking girl in the village and brought her back to America. Together, they worked long hours and raised two sons.

Gus still considered Anna the most beautiful girl in the world, and Anna still felt her heart do a little skip when Gus looked deep into her eyes and gave her a smile. Their only point of disagreement was their stubborn younger son, Michael.

"I'm sorry I can't be a perfect son for you, just like Deno," Michael yelled back at his father. "I didn't ask you to work so hard to establish two restaurants. You did it because you wanted to. I don't want to spend the rest of my life worrying about what other people want to eat. I want to live my own life and find out how the rest of the world lives. Greek Town in Chicago is not where I want to spend the rest of my life."

"You're worthless," his father shouted. "You'll end up in the gutter." Always the mediator, Anna stepped between her son and her husband. *They are so much alike. Their dark good looks and their quick temper,* she thought. "I wash my hands off you," continued Gus. "And, don't think you'll get any money from me."

That had been the end of it. Michael packed his clothes, and with a tearful goodbye to his mother, who slipped him some money—even though she knew that it was against her husband's wishes—he headed west. Unfortunately, making his fortune in Hollywood was not as easy as he expected. Real life wasn't like the fairy tales Anna read to him when he was a little boy.

Chapter 4

Finishing his drink at the bar, Michael slipped off the bar stool, and walked outside to the Savannah River. He leaned on the balustrade and looked at the dark, dirty water rushing toward the ocean. On his left, the Talmadge Bridge spanned across the river that separated Savannah from South Carolina. The bridge looked like an Erector set structure in the moonlight. Michael knew he had to make a decision. Someone from the mob would find him soon.

He was so deep in thought, he didn't notice the trio coming toward him until he heard Stephanie's drawl, "Why, here's the Yankee newcomer to our fair city. Guys, meet Michael Andrews, tall, dark, and dangerous."

Michael turned from the river to see Stephanie flanked by two men. An odd pair, one was tall and thin with red hair combed up in spikes. Tattoos filled all available space on his bare arms. He was dressed in tattered jeans and a sleeveless shirt. The other man had black dreadlocks trailing down his shoulders. He wore slim dark slacks, white dress shirt with rolled up sleeves, and expensive running shoes. Two sets of hoop earrings glinted in his ears.

Stephanie had an arm around the elbow of each man. She smiled crookedly at Michael and seemed unsteady on her feet.

"Oh, hi, Miss Boudreau," said Michael, thinking fast. "Your father thought I'd run into you. He asked me to give you a ride home."

"Hey," slurred Tattoo, "She's got her own wheels."

"Yeah," added Dreadlocks, "We ain't through partying yet."

Stephanie blinked and swayed slightly, her eyes fastened on Michael's intense turquoise ones. "Party's over, guys," said Michael as he slipped his arm around Stephanie's waist and led her toward the restaurant on the corner.

"Shit," said Tattoo. "Who's gonna buy our drinks now?"

Michael entered the restaurant with Stephanie stumbling along. He sat her down at the nearest table and ordered black coffee for both of them. The place was dim and almost empty. The lone bored-looking waitress shuffled to the coffee urn behind the counter and brought back two large white mugs. She pulled a towel out of her pocket and made a half-hearted swipe at the table. Before she could ask, Michael said, "Thank you, we won't need anything else."

"Well, aren't you Sir Galahad?" Stephanie smirked. "C'n take care of myself."

"You're not afraid someone will roll you over one night for the diamond rings you're wearing?" He gestured to the beautifully cut antique rings on her fingers.

"No one will touch Senator Boudreau's little girl," she laughed. "They're all 'fraid of him."

"I wouldn't be too sure," answered Michael. "Drugs and hunger can do strange things to a person. Where's your car?"

"Not sure. Think it's inna parking lot 'round here."

Michael wondered at his reaction to Stephanie. What was he feeling for this girl? Compassion? Attraction? There was a tightness in his loins. *It is just because you haven't had a woman in quite a while,* he told himself. He just wanted to get her safely home. "Drink your coffee and let's go find your car."

Finding Stephanie's car wasn't difficult. It was the red Mercedes convertible, illegally parked with a ticket on the windshield. "Daddy will take care of it," she scoffed.

The ride to Magnolia Bluff was uneventful. Michael kept his thoughts to himself and Stephanie dozed, her head pressed against the passenger door.

Lights were on inside the house and on the porch when they drove up. Maggie opened the door as soon as Michael stopped the car. "Why here's my old mammy," slurred Stephanie. "Bet she tells Daddy all about this at breakfast." Stephanie stumbled out of the car and into Maggie's arms. Maggie helped Stephanie inside, slamming the door in Michael's face, and turned off the lights.

Michael sat in the car a couple of minutes unsure what to do. *Hell*, he thought, *I'll just take this baby back to town with me.* He turned the Mercedes around in the circular driveway, let the top down and enjoyed the sounds and the smells of the beautiful spring night. He smiled to himself.

"Shit, I could get used to this car," he said. "Let's see how fast this baby can go."

Chapter 5

Early the next morning, Michael awoke to another glorious Savannah spring day. *Is it always so beautiful here,* he wondered. *Wouldn't take long to get used to t his climate.* He climbed into Stephanie's convertible and drove out to the Boudreau estate. The senator answered the door.

"Come in, come in and have some breakfast," he invited, leading Michael beyond the dining room to a large spotless kitchen. "I want to thank you for bringing Stephanie home last night. She would thank you herself if she weren't still sleeping."

Michael sat at the round table in the large, well-equipped kitchen. Maggie poured him coffee and brought a plate filled with eggs, ham, and grits. A large platter of biscuits was already on the table along with jam and butter.

"This looks and smells fantastic, Maggie." he said and attacked the food with gusto.

"Humpf," replied Maggie.

While Michael enjoyed the food, the senator had another cup of coffee and looked through the morning paper. Three biscuits and a clean plate later, Michael looked up sheepishly. "I didn't realize I was so hungry."

"Don't apologize," laughed Boudreau. "Maggie is a great

cook. Come into the study. We need to have another talk." The senator walked out of the kitchen expecting Michael to follow.

Michael sat there for a couple of minutes, trying to collect his thoughts. He still didn't know what to say to Boudreau. What the senator had proposed sounded good yesterday. This morning, he wasn't so sure. It would be a serious step with major consequences. Sure, he wanted the money, but didn't want to ruin his life with a loveless marriage, or ruin the life of an innocent girl.

Maggie whisked the plate from in front of him, giving him a look of disdain from dark, stormy eyes. Michael looked up, "You don't like me, do you?"

"I don't rightly know you, suh. I just don't know what you and the senator are cooking up for my baby. I've been taking care of her since she was little, when her mama died. She's already in trouble and she don't need somebody from up north giving her more misery."

Michael didn't have a reply. Folding his napkin, he got up from the table. "Thank you for the breakfast, Maggie." And he joined the senator in the study.

Boudreau sat behind his desk smoking one of his imported cigars. Michael took the chair he had vacated last night. *It's d*éjà vu, thought Michael. *What the hell am I doing here?*

The senator let out a long stream of smoke. "Michael, I've been thinking. The carriage house behind the garden is furnished and not in use. There's no reason for you to stay at a hotel. I'm sure a strong young man like you can make himself useful around here to earn his keep. Also, I spoke to my friend, the manager at the DeSoto Hotel. Seems like he can use a smart fella like you in his catering department. Think you can do that?"

Michael felt trapped, but he needed a job. His hotel bill was mounting and he had no way to pay it. "Senator," he said. "I would like a job and I do need a place to stay, but about the other..." He cleared his throat. "I just don't know. I need more time."

The senator lowered his head. "Unfortunately, there is no more time."

Fear seized Michael. "What do you mean? The guys at Vegas know I'm here?"

"No, no, that's not what I mean." Boudreau leaned back heavily in his chair. He took out another cigar, looked at it, rubbed his fingers around it, and then put it back in the humidor. "I didn't want to tell you this, but now I see it's necessary."

Boudreau swiveled his chair around and gazed out at the garden he loved so much. Through the window, he could see the bright morning sunshine glistening on the leaves of the trees and shrubs and the riot of color in the beds filled with early spring flowers. He rubbed his hand across his face and turned back to face Michael, his eyes unreadable. "I'm the one who doesn't have more time."

Michael stared at the senator, unable to comprehend what the older man was saying.

"Got the results of the tests from the doctor last week. I have lung cancer—the big C. The doctor's talking operation even though it's rather advanced. Got to admit I'm pretty scared. But, the worst part is what's going to happen to

Stephanie? Left by herself, the way she is, no telling what she'll do or who will take advantage of her."

Boudreau's voice was thick with emotion, his eyes shiny with unshed tears. He turned back to the window, unable to meet Michael's eyes.

Michael was shaken and felt a stab of compassion, yet at the same time couldn't help but think that this improved his position. Now, who was desperate? He didn't want to appear too anxious, but he could already taste the millions.

"I'm very sorry," he mumbled. "Why don't we just try it for a while with me living in the carriage house, getting to know Stephanie, and see how it goes?"

Boudreau cleared his throat. "All right, Maggie will show you the carriage house and then you need to go to the DeSoto and see the manager, Dave Pinkney, about that job." He turned back to the window, waving his hand in dismissal.

Chapter 6

Michael went back to the kitchen where Maggie had just finished cleaning up. "The senator said you would show me the carriage house."

"Lordy, this is getting even worse," she muttered. Without another look at Michael, she took a key from one of the kitchen cabinets and went out the back door into the garden. Michael followed.

The spacious garden was landscaped with flowering azaleas, roses, beds of annuals and small budding trees. In the middle of the garden was a goldfish pond and in front of the pond stood the most beautiful statue Michael had ever seen.

"My God, she's gorgeous," he exclaimed. "Aphrodite isn't it?" He went straight to the statue and put his hands on the marble expecting it to be cool to the touch. Surprisingly, he found it warm. He ran his hand up the arm of the statue to its shoulder and down the side to one thigh. The statue was positioned with one arm across the torso and the other reaching toward the classically beautiful face, which turned slightly over the right shoulder.

Hearing what sounded like a gasp from Maggie, Michael

turned to see a strange look on her face. She was clutching something she wore around her neck. "Is there something wrong?" he asked.

"No, just in a hurry. I got work to do, y' know."

Giving the statue a wide berth, she hurried to the carriage house at the end of the garden. Taking another look at the statue, Michael followed Maggie up a narrow stairway.

The carriage house apartment built over a double garage consisted of a living room-dining room combination, a small kitchen, and bedroom and bath. The furnishings were simple but tasteful. A sofa and one armchair with accompanying side tables and a small dining table with four chairs were grouped on a braided rug. Michael was glad to see the bed was large enough for his 6'1" frame and that the bath included a stall shower. There were fresh linens in the closet. There was no reason he couldn't be comfortable here.

Maggie dropped the key on the table and hurried back to the big house without a word. *She definitely doesn't like me*, thought Michael.

As Michael crossed the garden on his way back to the house, he paused and gazed admiringly at the statue of Aphrodite. "See you later, gorgeous," he whispered.

Michael found the senator in the study, still looking out at the garden. "I left my rental at the hotel when I brought back Stephanie's car. Can someone take me back to town?"

"Stephanie is going to a luncheon. She'll take you," answered Boudreau, without turning around. "She's in the kitchen having coffee. Let me know how the job interview comes out."

In the kitchen, Stephanie sat at the table having coffee

and toast. Michael thought she made a pretty picture in a royal blue dress that complimented her ivory skin. Her cloud of dark hair was piled high on her head with little wisps hanging down around her ears.

"Good morning, Stephanie. The senator says you're going to town. Can I have a ride?" Maggie looked up from the sink where she was washing dishes, and glared at Michael.

"Sure thing, I owe you a favor after last night." Stephanie finished her coffee, picked up her purse from the counter and walked outside where the convertible was parked. Michael, always the gentlemen, stepped ahead and opened the door for her.

Taking an exaggerated breath as she passed by him, he said, "My, my, you look and smell delicious this morning, Miss Stephanie." He went around and climbed in the passenger side.

Stephanie gave Michael a sideway glance as she drove the car toward the main road. "Look, about last night. Thank you for bringing me home. I admit was too groggy to drive, but I don't want you to get the idea that I need someone to take care of me because I can take care of myself. I have friends in town I could have stayed with."

"Yeah, I met a couple of your friends last night. I hope they weren't the pick of the litter."

"Oh, Mac and Jocko are okay," she laughed. "They don't mean any harm. What are you up to today?"

"I'm interviewing for a job at the DeSoto Hotel. Looks like I may be around for a while. Will that be a problem for you?"

"Why should a handsome guy be a problem? My

girlfriends will be wild to get their hands on you, Michael. You'll have to beat them off with a stick. Will that be a problem for you?"

"I've never run away from a woman in my life, but it depends on whose hands they are," he answered, looking pointedly at her pale slim hands on the steering wheel.

"Speaking of women," he continued, "I always get along with them no matter what their age, but Maggie doesn't seem to like me. Any reason why? Earlier when we were in the garden, she acted downright strange."

"Maggie is funny about the garden and the statue of Aphrodite. Her grandmother was Gullah and filled her head with all kinds of weird tales of spells and ghosts. She's very superstitious. Don't take it personally."

"My grandmother, Yiayia, was like that. When I was young, she would tell me stories about people in Greece who got sick and even died because someone put a curse on them. She worried that someone was going to put the 'evil eye' on me and pinned one of those little cloth amulets to my undershirt. When I was in middle school, the guys saw it when we were in P.E. and laughed at me. I had to beat up a couple of them to regain my status as a tough guy." He didn't admit to Stephanie he still carried that little incense filled cloth protector in his suitcase.

Chapter 7

That afternoon, Michael met with Dave Pinkney, the manager of the DeSoto Hotel. After no more than thirty minutes, he had the job, filled out the necessary forms and was told to report the next day at 9:00 a.m. As he was leaving, the manager shook his hand.

"Look here, Andrews, I don't mind doing a favor for the senator. His family and mine go way back, but you'll be expected to carry your weight around here or you'll be out the door in a New York minute."

Michael's eyes flashed blue fire, but he banked it quickly. He wanted to tell Pinkney to take his miserable little job and shove it, but he only smiled. "Thank you, sir, I understand." He quickly packed his bag, checked out of the hotel and drove back to Magnolia Bluff.

He parked his rental in the circular drive and carried his suitcase into the garden. A man wearing baggy jeans and a plaid shirt was pulling weeds in a corner. He stopped his work and stared at Michael. "I'm Michael Andrews, a friend of the family," he explained. The gardener nodded and went back to work. As Michael passed the statue of Aphrodite, he whispered, "Hello there, beautiful."

After unpacking his suitcase, taking a shower, and changing into casual slacks and polo shirt, Michael received a phone call from the senator inviting him to dinner. When he passed the statue of Aphrodite in the garden, he stopped short. This was odd. He was sure the statue was facing toward the driveway, but now it was facing the carriage house apartment. He shook his head. He must be mistaken.

He purposely came in through the kitchen door to speak to Maggie. It irritated him that she didn't like him. "Good evening, Maggie. Lucky me. I get to eat another of your wonderful meals tonight. I thought my grandmother was a great cook, but you're even better." Maggie gave him one of her dark piercing stares and went back to her work.

Michael shook his head and walked into the dining room to find the senator the only occupant at the table set for two. "Stephanie isn't eating with us tonight?" he asked, surprised to realize he was disappointed.

Boudreau shook his head. "No, she went out with her girlfriends. They're planning some kind of school reunion, I think. Well, how did it go at the hotel today?"

"It went very well and I start in the morning. I'll be in the catering department. Say, I want to ask you something about the statue in the garden. When I saw it earlier, it was facing the drive, but just now when I went by, it's facing the other way. Am I crazy here?"

Boudreau chuckled, "Now, don't you start. I hear enough about the statue being haunted from Maggie. José, the gardener, mentioned the base was loose. Must have turned it around when he repaired it."

After dinner, Michael walked back to his apartment. He

planned to turn in early to be rested for his first day of work, but around ten, he felt restless and decided to take a walk around the grounds. He walked down to the dock to take a look at the senator's sailboat. He could see it plainly in the glow of the floodlights. *Wow*, thought Michael, *this is not just a sailboat. It's a yacht.* It was a Hinckley custom made sloop. The name, '**Stephanie**' was painted in blue and gold letters on the bow.

When Michael heard the sound of a motor on the private road, he turned back toward the house and reached the front of the house just as Stephanie's car rolled into the driveway. He put out his cigarette and waited under the portico.

"Good evening," he said as she approached the door. Startled, Stephanie dropped the keys she was holding. Reaching quickly into her bag, she pulled out a mace container. "Hold it," he cried. "It's only me."

"What the hell are you doing slinking around in the dark? You scared me to death!" She was visibly shaken.

"I'm sorry; I didn't mean to frighten you." He stepped forward and took the can of mace out of her hand. Realizing she was trembling, he put his arms around her and gently rubbed her shoulders to calm her. "I was just taking a walk. Too restless to sleep." He bent down to look at her flushed face. "Are you okay now?"

Stephanie buried her face in Michael's strong shoulder. She could smell after shave lotion and something else, a sexy male scent. She put her arms around his waist to steady herself. Being in his arms felt – nice, comfortable.

Michael moved his lips down to her hair. It was jet black, thick and silky. She raised her head and his lips covered hers in a soft kiss. When Stephanie gave an involuntary sigh, he deepened the kiss, evoking an emotional response in her that both surprised and angered her.

As soon as she recovered her control, she pulled away and looked up at his dangerous turquoise eyes.

"Shame on you, big guy, for taking advantage of a girl when she's off balance."

Reluctantly, Michael released her. "You can't say you didn't enjoy it."

Her eyes were smoldering dark golden pools. "No, I can't say that."

Stephanie blinked as the portico light came on. Maggie opened the door with a smile for Stephanie and a scowl for Michael. She took Stephanie by the hand and pulled her into the house.

"Time for you to be in bed, Baby," she crooned. She picked up the keys from the threshold and slammed the door shut.

Michael walked into the garden and stopped by the statue of Aphrodite. He lit a cigarette and looked at the marble figure glowing in the moonlight. "You wouldn't give me the brush off, would you, beautiful?" He ran his hands over the statue's shoulders, waist and hip. "I could have sworn you were facing the other way yesterday."

Chapter 8

The next few weeks were busy for Michael. He made an effort to become familiar with his new job, which was mainly scheduling parties for the hotel. The salary was not what Michael was used to, but he didn't mind. He had a place to live and his eyes on the Boudreau millions.

Phillip Hargraves and Georgia Bennett were the other members of the catering department. Phillip, a Savannah native, lived with his mother in an old house in the historic district and had an associate degree in marketing from Armstrong State College. He was of medium height, slim, with straight brown hair that fell across his forehead. The large round glasses he wore gave him an owlish look. Phillip had intelligent brown eyes and a shy smile. It didn't take Michael long to figure out he was the senior member and the most knowledgeable in the office.

Georgia, who everyone called Peaches, was one of the many farm girls who flocked to Savannah from neighboring small towns. Usually, the girls were from large families and left home as soon as they received their high school diploma, either to get a job or find a husband in Savannah. Peaches had been in town for a year and lived with a girlfriend in a small apartment on Whitaker Street. She was blond, green-eyed and built like a man's favorite wet dream.

Michael recognized right away that he was in trouble on two fronts. When Peaches met him, her vivid green eyes widened and gave him a smile that was definitely a come-on. Being a healthy male, his body responded, but he knew Peaches had to be off-limits or she would jeopardize his chance with Stephanie. Then, almost immediately, he noticed the puppy dog look in Phillip's eyes when he stole glances at Peaches. *Damn*, he thought. *I have to watch my step here.*

For the next couple of days, Michael listened to Phillip explain the duties and the routine of the department. The job wasn't difficult or complicated but he listened quietly, trying to show Phillip that he understood he was the senior man in order to win his friendship.

Peaches did everything she could to get his attention. She batted her sexy emerald eyes and stood close to him every chance she got. One day, when he was sitting at his desk, she leaned over to hand him some papers and presses her substantial breasts to his back. Instantly aroused, he jumped up and ran into the restroom. Phillip followed to find Michael splashing cold water on his face and trying to get his libido under control.

Phillips eyes were troubled. "What just happened out there? Peaches ran into the ladies room crying." He looked accusingly at Michael. "I don't want her hurt."

It was obvious to Michael that Phillip cared for Peaches so much he didn't want her unhappy even if it meant being with another man. Michael thought quickly.

"Hell, Phillip, Peaches is a gorgeous girl. A man can

get all steamed up being around her. I don't want to hurt her feelings, but you see, man, I'm committed to another woman and Peaches would complicate matters. She thinks so highly of you. Why don't you take her to lunch and explain everything to her."

"You really think she likes me?" Phillip looked hopefully at Michael. "I've always wanted to ask her out, but she's so beautiful and has so many boyfriends…"

"That may be so, but you're different. She looks up to you and she needs a friend right now. Ask her out to lunch. Tell her she is beautiful, hold her hand and say you want to be her friend. Tell her she doesn't need someone like me to mess up her life."

Meanwhile, Peaches was in the ladies room with her friend Linda, the restaurant cashier, wiping her eyes and freshening her makeup. Peaches was more angry than hurt.

"I saw that flat-chested Stephanie Boudreau come by and give that gorgeous hunk the fish eye. Nobody flips me off like that. What does she have that I don't have?"

"Oh honey," replied Linda, patting Peaches on the back. "What she's got is her daddy's money."

Phillip took Peaches to lunch. When they came back, Peaches wouldn't look at Michael but Phillip had a smile on his face. It was awkward in the office for a couple of days but pretty soon the incident was forgotten and Peaches and Phillip left together almost every day after work.

Michael was surprised to find that he enjoyed his job. His knowledge about food, acquired when he reluctantly helped his father in the family restaurant, won over the chef and the kitchen staff. His good looks and natural charm attracted the middle–aged ladies that planned parties or wedding receptions for their daughters. Word about the improved services in the catering department reached the hotel manager, and all three got a small raise. The trio had melded into a productive working unit.

Chapter 9

Since Stephanie was busy with plans for the Savannah Country Day School reunion, the senator invited Michael to eat with him almost every night. Boudreau was lonesome and Michael liked having dinner in the formal dining room with flickering candlelight, fancy china, and flowers on the table. Of course, the food was always delicious.

They spoke of many things. Michael told the senator about his job and he listened when the older man gave him advice. When he felt more comfortable with the senator, Michael tried to explain his complicated relationship with his father.

The senator told stories about Savannah's rich history, the coming of General Oglethorpe and the reason for the unique squares that brought the city of Savannah tourist dollars each year. Boudreau reminded Michael that he was welcome to use the sailboat anytime he wished.

At first, Boudreau worried that in his anxiety about his health and concern about Stephanie, he'd made a mistake about Michael. However, after a while he decided he liked the boy and discovered that there was a good, solid core hidden beneath the rough edges, especially when Michael spoke of his family. Although it was on both their minds, the one subject they both avoided was the senator's health.

Michael mentioned to Boudreau that he was aware that Maggie was unhappy to see him in the house so often, but the senator said, "Don't worry about it, Michael. She's very protective of Stephanie, but she'll get used to you."

One evening when Stephanie was home for dinner, the senator suggested that she take Michael out on the boat. "I promised the boy a ride on my new sailboat. Why not take him out this Saturday? Maggie can pack you a picnic lunch."

"I'd love to go if Stephanie isn't too busy." Michael jumped at the chance to be alone with Stephanie since things between them were not moving as fast as he liked.

"I think I can arrange to be free this Saturday," smiled Stephanie.

"Why not take him to Bradley Point on Ossabaw Island? It's a long trip, but the tides will be perfect. The high spring tide will carry you out in the morning, and in the afternoon the strong incoming tide will get you home before dark," said the senator.

Chapter 10

Saturday morning broke clear and sunny. Maggie reluctantly handed Michael a basket of fried chicken, potato salad, biscuits, fruit, and chocolate cake. Ice tea and beer completed the picnic meal.

Michael waited for Stephanie under the front portico. When she arrived, they walked around the left side of the house to the dock. Michael wore bathing trunks and a t-shirt. He couldn't help but admire Stephanie's long legs beneath white shorts and a bright red halter. She carried a large cloth bag full of towels and other bathing items. They both had on canvas shoes. Michael reached for Stephanie's hand as they walked toward the dock. He hid a little smile when she didn't pull her hand away.

As they approached the boat, Michael noticed the water, a muddy green color, almost covered the tall slender grasses of the salt marsh. A high spring tide, Boudreau had called it. Thousands of fiddler crabs skittered about, the males waving one large claw in the air, displaying their anger at being disturbed. Nearby, a Great Blue Heron waded in the shallows, making a meal of mud minnows. Farther down the shore, a lone alligator glided silently through the water-logged grasses in search of his breakfast.

A strong smell of salt, sulphur, and decaying plant and animal matter assailed Michael's nostrils. When he stopped and sniffed, Stephanie looked him and laughed, "You're smelling the southern salt marsh. Those of us who grew up around water hardly notice it. To me, it smells like home. Unfortunately, on top of that we're getting a whiff of the paper mill about 15 miles away on the Savannah River. Now, that I never get used to, but it means jobs to a lot of folks in the Savannah area."

Michael laughed in return, "Well, it's a pretty strong odor for someone not used to it, but I'll take it if I can sail on this boat. Wow, it's a beauty. I only saw it at night before."

The bright southern sun shimmered on the custom built yacht, a Hinckley 42' sloop. The bronze hardware and teak decks gleamed like gold and the blue painted hull reflected the ripples on the water. The spars were carbon fiber with roller furling sails, designed for easy sail handling by one person. "I see she's built long and lean with curves in the right places, just like her namesake," he said with a grin.

"Yes, it is a nice boat," she agreed as Michael helped her onto the yacht and handed her the picnic basket. "Daddy couldn't wait to get it, but now for some reason, he seems to have lost interest in sailing," she said with a puzzled little frown. "Let's take the picnic things below to the galley."

The galley was small, but had a full kitchen with a refrigerator filled with food and drinks, a freezer, and an icemaker. Cabinets and a small table made of teak and other tropical woods glowed like warm honey.

Although Michael had sailed Lasers and Lightnings in college, he had never been on a yacht like this, so Stephanie showed him around the boat. They checked the engine and started the Yanmar 30hp diesel to let it warm up. Stephanie flipped on the VHF radio, depth finder and color GPS chart plotter. Together, they removed the sail covers and she showed Michael how the sail control systems worked.

Michael was impressed with Stephanie's nautical knowledge. "Where did you learn all this?" he asked. "You're really good."

"Mostly from Daddy, but I also had several summers of sailing instruction at the Savannah Yacht Club."

Now ready to get underway, they untied the dock lines, and eased away from the dock with Michael at the helm. Stephanie removed the dock lines and fenders and stowed them below.

"Time for some sail. Just hold her in the middle of the creek," she called out, as she hoisted the mainsail. The spinnaker ballooned up toward the cerulean blue sky and filled with air, lifting the boat to an additional 6 knots. When Stephanie shut down the diesel, there was an abrupt absence of noise, and the only sound discernible was the soft sigh of water racing along the hull and wind in the sails.

They all but flew southeast with the tide down Grove River until it merged with the Forrest River at Rose Dhu Island, then turned south until the Forrest River merged with Little Ogeechee. Another slight turn to the east brought them into the Intracoastal Waterway at Green Island Sound. The boat was moving faster as they sailed toward the sea.

Stephanie pointed out the sights along the way, remnants of Native-American villages, Revolutionary War forts, Civil War forts, and told him stories about blockade runners, rum runners, and moonshine stills.

"Look, that's Green Island. The confederates build dirt forts and earthen works there, trying to stop Sherman's march to the sea."

"That's interesting. Being from the Chicago area, I had no idea the Georgia coast was so full of history," said Michael." You amaze me. Not only can you captain a yacht, you know enough history to be a teacher."

"Well, I should," she answered. "I do have a degree in education even though I have never used it."

Soon, Ossabaw Island at Bradley Point was in sight and they sped toward it, the yacht running like a race horse towards the sea. Michael didn't know a sailboat could move this fast. They sailed up to the beach at Bradley Point and selected a spot to drop anchor. Stephanie pushed the button on the electronic windlass, releasing the anchor with a splash and clatter of chain.

Michael was swamped with emotions he did not understand, the incredible boat, the fantastic view of water, marsh and sky, the beautiful Stephanie beside him. He couldn't remember ever being so happy and content, so peaceful and in tune with nature. His fears about Las Vegas, his resentment of his father, his confusion about his future all faded away. This is where he wanted to be. Somehow, he felt he belonged in this lazy, hazy, smelly part of the world.

When Stephanie glanced at Michael, he looked a bit dazed. "Michael," she said, putting her hand on his arm. "Are you ready for lunch or would you like to swim out to the beach and take a little walk first?" *Why was he so quiet,* she wondered.

Startled by her voice, Michael pulled back from his

thoughts. "Yeah, let's take a walk on the beach. It looks fantastic." He took off his t-shirt and Stephanie slipped off her shorts, revealing a matching red bikini bottom. Together they dove into the water.

An hour later, back on the deck and wrapped in thick terry cloth towels, they spread the picnic lunch on a small table and enjoyed the food Maggie had prepared. Both had worked up tremendous appetites and were surprised when there was practically nothing left to put back into the basket.

"Do I have to fight you for that last piece of cake?" teased Michael. "I can't believe a skinny girl like you can eat so much."

"Who are you calling skinny?" she laughed. "No one has ever called me that before. If you think I'm too thin, you must like your women voluptuous."

He gave her the full power of his laser blue eyes as they raked over her from head to toe. "No," he said. "I like my women exactly like you." She was surprised to feel such heat from his look, all the way from the blush on her face to her belly and farther down to her inner core.

After lunch, Stephanie stretched out on one of the deck chairs. Her pale ivory skin turned golden in the sun light. She put her head back and closed her eyes. The sun was a warm blanket and she slipped into a dream—to another time, another place.

Michael watched Stephanie as she slept. God, she was lovely. Her slim body in repose was like a statue, but instead of cold and white she was warm and golden. He could see the pulse beating at her throat that proved she was a real live woman. He ached to touch her, to feel that pulse, but she looked so vulnerable. He didn't want to disturb her, just wanted to touch her. She turned her head and made a little sound of discomfort.

Thinking she was having a bad dream, he sat down next to her and gently put his hand on her shoulder. Stephanie started and her eyes snapped open. "Hi," he said, quietly. "Bad dream?"

Her hazel eyes, like deep golden pools, looked back at him sadly. "I wish it was just a bad dream," she said. And because she could see compassion in his eyes, she told him about Spencer. She couldn't believe how it all just poured out, all the pain of the betrayal.

Afterwards, she was embarrassed. "Sorry to drop all that on you. I don't know what made me do it."

"That's okay." He took her hands and kissed her fingers. His incredible eyes looked deep into hers. "I think he was a fool to let you go." He reluctantly pulled his eyes away from Stephanie and toward the water. "The tide has turned. Let's go home."

They set the sails, pushed the button to raise the anchor, and sailed home with the incoming tide. They wouldn't need the engine again until it is time to dock.

The rest of the afternoon passed in a pleasant manner. Michael entertained Stephanie with stories of his boyhood in Chicago, and she, in turn, told him about growing up in Savannah. By the time they reached the dock, Stephanie opinion of Michael had changed considerably. Somehow, during the boat ride they had become friends.

When Michael walked her to the door of the house, he reached up to touch a wisp of hair that had fallen across her cheek and put it behind her ear. Stephanie felt her pulse race.

He put his arms around her and leaned down to kiss her forehead. When she closed her eyes and raised her face to his, Michael lightly brushed is lips across hers, turned and went into the garden, leaving her wanting.

Chapter 11

After the sailboat ride, Stephanie had dinner with her father and Michael a couple of times a week. Sometimes after dinner, Michael took her for a ride in her convertible or they shared a box of popcorn at the movies.

"Do you mind, Senator, if I take this beautiful girl out for a while?" he would ask.

"No, you youngsters go ahead. I have some reading to do. Have a good time." The senator was happy that Stephanie was not hanging around the fast crowd in the bars down on River Street any more. Her eyes were clearer and her appetite had improved.

Once when they were out, Stephanie wondered out loud, "Maybe I should stay home with Daddy more. He seems a little peaked these days. He's quiet and doesn't seem to have an appetite. You see him quite a bit. Have you noticed anything?"

He didn't know what to say. Michael knew about the senator's cancer, but it was not his place to reveal the secret to Stephanie. Instead, he changed the subject, "What would you like to do this evening, ride to the beach or go downtown?"

Michael was very careful with Stephanie on their nights

out. He held her hand, put his arm round her shoulders and kissed her cheek in a brotherly way. Later after he arrived home, he took a cold shower. Experiencing feelings of repressed desire of her own, Stephanie wondered why he didn't really kiss her.

After several dates, they become very easy with each other, laughing and joking and telling each other about their awkward teenage years.

"Of course, you never had any awkward years," teased Stephanie, giving him a sideways look under her long dark lashes. "I'll bet the girls were after you from the age of ten."

"Why that's not true at all. I was all of twelve the first time a girl grabbed me and gave me a big sloppy kiss. She was older, about fourteen, I think. That woke me up in more ways than one."

Stephanie laughed and held up her hand, palm out. "Please don't describe the ways. I get the picture. I guess we're a bit slower down south, or maybe it's because I'm a girl. I didn't have my first crush until I was thirteen. It was with Scotty McIntire. I liked him because he was best at kick ball in my class and had blond hair and sparkling blue eyes.

"My best friend, Ginger, liked him, too. Scotty almost broke us up, but we managed to stay good friends, especially after Scotty dropped us both the next year for the school slut, Rhoda Morgan. Our friendship really cemented then, because we could both hate Rhoda. Now, I wonder why we didn't hate Scotty?"

It was Michael's turn to laugh. Being with Stephanie was no hardship. She was smart and funny, a good listener, not to mention gorgeous with those sexy eyes and graceful slim but curvy body. He was having a hard time keeping his hands off her, but he didn't want to move too fast and ruin the friendship that had become important to him.

Chapter 12

"So girlfriend, how's it going with tall, dark and sexy?" Ginger asked Stephanie one day, while having lunch at the Pink House on Reynolds Square.

"Gosh, Ginger, I was afraid of Michael when we first met, but now we've become good friends. However, I wish he would stop being such a nice guy and grab me and lay one on me - like the kiss he gave me the night he brought me home from River Street."

"Well, why are you being such a shy violet? You said you haven't decided who to ask to the dance at the Oglethorpe Club. Ask Michael. We're all dying to meet this Greek God you keep talking about."

"I'm not shy," said Stephanie picking at her crab salad. I'm cautious because I'm attracted to Michael. You know what happened the last time I got tangled up with a guy."

"How well I remember," said Ginger, looking at the dessert menu. "But, Spencer was slime. Give this guy a break. Don't make up your mind until you know him better."

"That's the problem. I'd like to know more about his background. Ever since our sailboat ride, our relationship has changed, which has surprised us both. The times we've been out together, he's been a perfect gentleman, yet I think there's more to his visit to Savannah than he lets on. I suspect Daddy is somehow involved and planning something with Michael but I'm not sure what it is."

"Gee, Steffie, you have to stop looking for mysteries. Take a chance and get back into life. As for myself, I'm going to take a chance and order a piece of cheesecake and hope it doesn't attach itself to my butt."

When she finished her cheesecake, Ginger gave Stephanie a hug and went back to her mother's real estate office, where she had made herself invaluable as a top-notch real estate agent. Both men and woman clients loved her ability to find the best house for the least amount of money. It didn't hurt that she had a bouncy personality and a sunny smile.

Not having a job to rush to, Stephanie lingered over coffee, and let her thoughts drift back to college and the events that had changed her life.

Smith College, Northampton, MA   1971

"What's wrong with you, girl?" Ginger gave her friend a disgusted look. "That blond Adonis picked you out from the whole group at the dance and you turned him down. I'd go out with him in a minute. I hear he's going to be a lawyer and comes from money. He's a senior and they don't usually look at lowly sophomores."

"Oh, I don't know. If he's a senior, he'll soon be gone so what's the point? I'm not interested in getting into anything serious," answered Stephanie, as she put down the book she was reading and stretched her arms over her head.

"Jesus, Stef, If I looked like you, I'd be out every night." Letting her sparkling green eyes roam over her friend, she admired the slim dark haired girl stretched across the twin bed in their dorm room. Ginger was a little envious of Stephanie's long raven black hair, striking hazel eyes and porcelain white skin. Beneath Stephanie's straight nose was a sensuous mouth. Her heart shaped face ended with a chin graced with a small cleft.

Stephanie smiled at her roomie and best friend. "I haven't noticed any lack of male companionship in your life." Ginger was petite, curvaceous, and bubbly. Her crown of red curls complimented her bouncy personality.

"Yes, but I have to work at it. All you have to do is stand there with that pouty mouth and those big doe eyes and you strike the guys dumb. And, you're still a virgin, for heaven's sake. I lost my innocence at the first freshman mixer. And I'm not a bit sorry. I'm here to spend Daddy's money and have a good time. Getting a degree is just a by-product."

"Honey, you were never innocent. How about all those times we double dated back home in Savannah? You and your boyfriend of the week had the car rocking and I had to listen to all that moaning and groaning coming from the back seat."

"Stef, you know that was just kid stuff. I never went all the way. My mama would've killed me. That's why I wanted us to go off to college, away from home, far from Savannah, so we could cut loose. I'll have fantastic memories of my college days. What will you remember? Just those stupid 'A's you keep getting?"

"Now, let's talk seriously. What are you going to do about Mr. Spencer Whittier Stockton III? He's too big a fish to toss back so I'm gonna help you reel him in."

As it turned out, Stephanie didn't need any help from her friend except encouragement. Spencer set his sights on Stephanie and wooed her with both patience and determination. By the time Stephanie graduated, he had finished law school and given her a huge diamond engagement ring.

Mr. and Mrs. Stockton were friendly and polite but Stephanie was never quite sure how they felt about her, even though they gave parties at their palatial home to introduce her to their friends. Spencer's father was a distinguished gray-haired older version of her fiancé. His mother was a tall thin woman with a carefully made up face, always dressed in expensive designer clothes. Mrs. Stockton had a way of looking down her patrician nose at Stephanie that made her feel uncomfortable. When Stephanie voiced her concern to Spencer, he assured her that his parents liked her very much and were delighted to have her in the family.

Stephanie was dazzled by Spencer's attention, by the gifts and the parties. "I feel like Cinderella," she confided to her best friend. "But I'm afraid the clock will strike twelve and I will turn into a pumpkin."

"Don't be ridiculous," answered Ginger. "Spencer's crazy about you. He looks at you like he could swallow you whole in just one bite. I can see he's gorgeous, but tell me the important stuff, how is he in bed?"

Stephanie's cream complexion turned pink. "Oh, making love with him is wonderful. He's so careful and patient with me. He treats me like a china doll and doesn't want to hurt me."

Ginger was surprised at Stephanie's answer. She thought Mr. Stockton III would show a little more passion, but she assumed that he realized that Stephanie was inexperienced and didn't want to frighten her.

Mr. and Mrs. Stockton's visit to Savannah to meet the senator did not go well. It was obvious Mrs. Stockton had expected the Boudreau mansion to be more like Tara and couldn't believe their only servant was Maggie. The Stocktons were certainly not impressed with downtown Savannah, where several Broughton Streets stores were boarded up and empty. Mrs. Stockton turned up her nose at the historic houses, some deserted and in need of repair and hunched like specters around unkempt squares.

Looking at her beloved city with new eyes, Stephanie could see that Broughton Street did look shabby. River Street reconstruction was still underway, and many previously beautiful mansions were unoccupied. Sadly, some were reduced to rooming houses or tenements.

Boudreau was his charming and hospitable self, but after Mr. and Mrs. Stockton left, he was very quiet. Finally, he asked, "Stephanie, honey, do you love this man? He seems like a fine person, but I'm not sure his parents are our kind of people."

"Oh yes, Daddy," she replied, her eyes shining with happiness. "Spencer is wonderful. We love each other very much. Spencer agrees his family is a bit stuffy, but it's just the way they were raised. We won't have to live with them." *Thank heaven*, she added to herself.

Afterward, Stephanie couldn't remember exactly when the fairytale began to crumble. Maybe it was after Mr. and

Mrs. Stockton visited Savannah. Or maybe it was when Spencer began to work longer hours at his father's law office while Stephanie sat alone in the apartment they rented to be their first home.

Stephanie was sure something was wrong when Spencer told her his mother suggested they wait a few months to get married since he was so busy and distracted by his work. Alone until late each night and confused by his change toward her, Stephanie began to drink herself to sleep. When that wasn't enough, she added sleeping pills.

One day, she decided to visit Spencer at his office and invite him to lunch. His secretary told her he was lunching at a nearby restaurant. When Stephanie reached the restaurant, she saw Spencer sitting at a secluded table holding hands with an attractive blond. When Stephanie confronted him that evening, he admitted that he was seeing his old girlfriend who had moved back to town. When he confessed that he was unsure about their coming marriage, Stephanie threw the diamond engagement ring at him, packed her bags and moved into a hotel.

In deep depression, she continued to drink and take pills. For days, Stephanie moved as if under water, unable to concentrate, unable to process what had happened. She wanted to go home to Savannah but didn't know what to say to her father.

Ginger was the one who found her passed out in her room, took her to the hospital and called the senator. Doctors at the hospital confirmed her deep depression along with dehydration and loss of weight. After two months of therapy, she came back to Savannah looking more like herself, except she was thinner and had a lost look in her beautiful hazel eyes.

Savannah   1976

"Can I get you something else, Miss Boudreau?"

The voice of the waitress at The Pink House brought Stephanie back to the present. "No, thank you. Sorry I stayed so long." She smiled apologetically and left a large tip on the table.

When she went outside to get into her car, she was surprised there was no ticket on her windshield even though the parking meter had run out. Stephanie considered this a good omen. As she drove home, she talked to herself. *Ginger was right. She had to climb out of this funk and find something useful to do with her life. But, what?*

Her question was answered the next morning.

Chapter 13

"Good Morning, Stephanie." The voice on the telephone was familiar, *but who…?* "This is Amanda Boatwright. How are you? I hope I'm not calling too early."

"Oh, Dr. Boatwright, I'm okay. It's so good to hear from you."

Dr. Amanda Boatwright was Stephanie's favorite teacher when she was a student at Savannah Country Day Academy. Amanda was young and attractive and related to the teenagers better than most of the older instructors. She inspired Stephanie to seriously consider becoming a teacher. Of course Stephanie's life had not gone as planned with the breakup with Spencer, and now two years after college graduation, she was still confused about what she wanted to do with the rest of her life.

"I was glad to hear that you were in town," continued Amanda. I remembered how much you enjoyed our class and how you were considering teaching. I'm head mistress of the lower school at Country Day now and I really need your help. Mrs. Strong, our third grade teacher, is pregnant and isn't due until after school is out for the summer. Unfortunately, she's having some problems and her doctor has prescribed complete bed rest until the baby is born. Would you be willing to substitute for her class for the rest of the school year?"

Stephanie was surprised Dr. Boatwright would ask her to do this. She didn't think she had the background or the experience to take over a class of children.

"I don't think so, Dr. Boatwright. My degree is in education but I don't have a teaching certificate."

"It's only for six weeks and you don't need a certificate to substitute. Of course, if you decide to come back, you could get your certificate this summer at Armstrong. I know you can do it. You were my best student and you talked about teaching all the time. Besides, I checked at Smith and the head of the education department remembered you. She said you received one of the highest grades in your class when you did your practice teaching. I'm convinced you can do this. The real question is, do you want to do it?"

Stephanie rubbed her eyes and ran a hand through her long dark hair. "Honestly, Dr. Boatwright, I'm flattered you've asked me and that you have trust in me, but I haven't done much of anything for the past couple of years. I don't think I can do it because…uh…you see…I…um…"

"Stephanie, why don't you consider this an opportunity to see if teaching is for you? Come to the school and visit the class. The teacher's aide has been holding down the fort, but frankly, she's out of her depth. Come to my office after nine tomorrow morning and we'll talk about it. The children need someone like you and you may find that you like it."

Dr. Boatwright didn't add that one of the reasons she called was she heard from friends that Stephanie looked lost and was hanging around River Street bars.

After she hung up the phone, Stephanie sat on her bed and looked across the room into the mirror on top of her dressing table. She didn't like what she saw. Her eyes were dull from the pills she had taken last night to help her sleep. Her face was pale as chalk and her shoulders drooped. Maybe it was time to stop feeling sorry for herself and think of helping someone else. Dr. Boatwright sounded as if she really needed her. The professor had been very kind to her when she was in school. Maybe it was time to give back.

When she went downstairs, Stephanie found the senator in his study sitting behind his desk, his head in his hands. The heavy drapes at the window had not been opened leaving the room in semi-darkness. There was an eerie chill in the room, even though it was a warm spring day outside.

"Daddy, is something wrong?"

Startled by his daughter's voice, he looked up and forced a smile on his face. "No, honey, everything is fine. I was just thinking. Are you going out or can you come in and talk with me for a while?"

Stephanie stepped to the double window behind the desk and pulled open the drapes, revealing the garden resplendent in colorful spring flowers. Morning sun streaked into the room bringing light and warmth to the polished wood furniture and the muted colors of the Turkish carpet.

"That's better," she said and sat down in the chair in front of the senator's desk. A tray with a carafe of coffee and two cups sat on a small side table. Stephanie smiled when she recognized the blue and white ceramic mugs she had given Boudreau last Father's Day. The senator hated drinking coffee from a small dainty cup. "Can I pour you some coffee, Daddy?"

"Yes, if you'll have some with me. I'm really fine," he said, realizing that Stephanie was still inspecting him carefully. "Just a bit of spring fever, I guess. Did you want something in particular or did you just want to spend some time with your old father?"

"As a matter of fact, I do have something to tell you. And, you're not old, Senator Boudreau." She got up and hugged his neck and gave him a kiss on his cheek. "You are a handsome man. Don't think I haven't noticed women looking at you. Maybe you should look back. But, that's a subject for another day."

Stephanie filled the two mugs with coffee, handed one to her father, and returned to her chair. "Daddy, I don't know if you remember my favorite teacher at Country Day, Dr. Amanda Boatwright. She's now head of the lower school. She called me this morning to ask me to substitute for a third grade teacher who can't finish out the year. At first I told her no, but she asked me to come to the school and discuss it further. I'm thinking I need something to do, something to pull me out of the doldrums I've been in. I don't really feel qualified, but, she wants me anyway. What do you think? Do you think I can do it?"

"Of course, you can do it. All those good grades you received at school proved how smart you are. But, it's not just that, you've always loved children and they have always responded to you. This is a wonderful idea and it's perfect for you. By all means, go and see Dr. Boatwright. She wouldn't have called you if she didn't think you have the requirements for the position."

Boudreau got up and put his arm around his daughter's

waist and walked her to the door of his study. "Now, go to the kitchen and ask Maggie to make you a nice breakfast. Remember? I always insisted on your having a good breakfast before you went to school when you were little. This is the same thing, isn't it?"

Stephanie kissed his cheek again and smiled, "Okay Daddy, a good breakfast it is."

The senator stood at the door and watched his daughter walk down the hall. "Thank God," he whispered.

Chapter 14

Two weeks later, Stephanie sat behind a desk in a classroom at Country Day School. Her students were in the lunchroom with Linda, the aide, giving her a half-hour to catch up on paper work. Instead of correcting papers, she leaned her chin on her hand and looked around the classroom, remembering how easy it had been to settle in with this group of children. They were very bright and their teacher had prepared them well. All she had to do was review the subjects they were to be tested on before the end of the school year.

Stephanie was sure they would all pass, except for Lonnie. She didn't know what to do about him. Lonnie sat in the back of the room and refused to do his work. His records indicated that his intelligence was above average and he had made good grades until recently. The previous teacher had not left any information in Lonnie's file to explain the change in his grades or his behavior. Not only did he not do his work, but he picked fights with the other children if they tried to talk to him. Stephanie thought he may miss his teacher and tried to comfort him, but he gave her an angry look and turned his head away. Realizing she needed help with Lonnie, she had asked the school counselor, Mrs. Abbot, to meet with her today.

"Hi," said Rose Abbot as she walked into the classroom carrying a folder. "What seems to be the problem with Lonnie Spalding? There's nothing in his file but good comments. He makes good grades and gets along with the other kids. His parents come to every parent-teacher conference and are supportive of school activities."

"Well, it must be that he misses Mrs. Strong or he doesn't like me," said Stephanie. "All the other students have accepted me except for Lonnie. I just have to try a little harder with him. I don't want his dislike of me to influence his grades. I'll have a little talk with him this afternoon after school. He may be concerned about Mrs. Strong. I'll reassure him that she is doing well. If this is the case, maybe I could ask his mother to take him to visit her."

"That's not a bad idea, but let me call his mother first. Things were a little crazy the last couple of days before Mrs. Strong had to leave. She's a top-notch teacher, but she may have missed something. I'll call Lonnie's house tonight and let you know in the morning what I find out."

Later that evening, Stephanie was sitting at the kitchen table correcting papers and talking with Maggie when the senator came in. "Well, well, how's the new teacher getting along?" Leaning over, he kissed his daughter's cheek.

"Pretty good except for one little guy who is giving me trouble. I think it's because he misses Mrs. Strong and doesn't seem to like me."

"What?" he said in mock alarm. "Can't believe that. All the boys in school liked you. Do you want me to beat up his father?" Boudreau was pleased to see the change in Stephanie since she started teaching. She wasn't staying out late at night and she seemed happy.

"No, I don't think that will be necessary," smiled Stephanie. "The school counselor is calling his parents tonight to find if there is something going on at home causing the boy to be unhappy at school. But, thanks for wanting to be my knight in shining armor. We'll get to the bottom of it."

The next morning, Stephanie arrived at school early to meet with the counselor. She found Mrs. Abbot in her office eating a bagel and drinking coffee. "Come in, Stephanie. Would you like the other half of this bagel? I find it easier to pickup breakfast on the way to work instead of making something at home."

"Thanks, but Maggie and Daddy won't let me leave the house without a full breakfast each morning. Tell me, have you found out anything that will help me with Lonnie?"

"Yes, I have, but give me a few minutes to finish my breakfast," she said around a mouthful of bagel and cream cheese.

Stephanie curbed her impatience by looking around the small room that served as the lower school counselor's office. Shelves on three walls were filled with books and boxes of student records. The door, front and back, was used as a bulletin board covered with children's art work. A child-size table with one small chair was placed in a corner with several games and puzzles arranged on a low shelf close by. The single high window looked out into the school playground. The only personal item in the office was a framed picture of Rose Abbot and her husband.

The counselor finished her coffee and set down the cup. "I'm afraid I don't have good news," she said. "Two weeks ago, just about the time you took over the class, Lonnie's mother fell down the stairs in their home. In fact, it was Lonnie who called 911. She was taken to the hospital and has not regained consciousness. Mr. Spalding is devastated and has spent day and night at the hospital. The doctors have no idea when, or if, she will wake up. Lonnie and his one-year-old sister have been in the care of an aunt that Lonnie doesn't know very well. No wonder Lonnie is confused and upset."

"Oh, my. This is way beyond my area of expertise. The poor little boy." Stephanie's tender heart ached for Lonnie. "What can I do to help him?"

Mrs. Abbot shook her head, "I suggest we schedule a session for Lonnie with me every day. He needs someone to talk with right now. As for your part, have patience with him. Don't press him for his school work. Be aware of his moods and if he seems particularly upset, send him to me. If you can step in and diffuse any problems with the other kids, that will help. Let's not say anything to the other children right now. Telling the rest of the class might upset Lonnie even more."

For the next week, Lonnie reluctantly went to the counselor's office each day. Mrs. Abbot reported to Stephanie that he would not talk about the accident and would only answer her questions with a yes or no. She suggested that Stephanie try to talk to him. "It can't hurt," she said.

Stephanie didn't have a clue how to approach Lonnie, but during lunch period a few days later, she had the opportunity. Linda, the teacher's aide, brought Lonnie into the classroom, holding his arm with one hand and carrying Lonnie's lunchbox in the other.

"Miss Boudreau, this is the third day that Lonnie won't eat any of his lunch and I thought maybe you could talk to him." Lonnie jerked his arm away and looked down at his sneakers.

"Thank you, Miss Linda. Since I haven't eaten my sandwich yet, Lonnie and I can have lunch together." Linda shook her head and walked back to the lunchroom.

Stephanie's thoughts were in turmoil. *What to say to this troubled child? Maybe he just needed a quiet place to eat.* "Here, let's use my desk as our table." She moved the majority of the papers and reached in the bottom drawer for a bag of paper plates and napkins. Opening up the napkins to use a placemats, she handed Lonnie the plates and plastics forks so he could set the table.

At first, Lonnie just looked at the plates and forks. He blinked to keep from crying, then carefully placed the paper plates and forks on the make-shift placemats. He looked at Stephanie, his big brown eyes filled with pain. "I always helped my Mommy set the table. She taught me how to put the forks and spoons in the right place." His voice trembled and big fat tears rolled down his freckled cheeks.

Instinctively, Stephanie went down on her knees and gathered him in her arms while he sobbed his heart out, soaking her blouse. She held him close, rubbed his back and murmured, "There, there. It's okay, it's okay to cry. Everything will be all right." She continued to hold him until his heavy breathing and hiccups subsided. Only then, she sat in her chair and pulled him onto her lap.

BESS T. CHAPPAS

"Lonnie, I know you are worried about your mother, but you have to believe that she will get better. Why, you're a hero. I heard that you called 911. Your Dad must be proud that you knew what to do to get your mother help right away."

A stricken look came over Lonnie's face and the tears began anew. He hid his face in Stephanie's shoulder. "No, no, no," he cried. "It's my fault that Mommy is hurt. It's my fault because I was a bad boy and she tripped on the laundry and fell down the stairs."

Stephanie wasn't sure she had heard correctly. What could he mean? She continued to hold him close for a few minutes before she pulled back.

"Lonnie, what do you mean it's your fault that your mother is hurt? Can you tell me what happened? You did call 911 didn't you?"

"Yes, I did, but Mommy asked me to go upstairs to check on my sister, Betsy, and I didn't want to because I was watching TV. Betsy was crying and crying and Mommy ran up the steps carrying a basket of laundry and she tripped and fell. If I had gone upstairs like she asked me, she wouldn't be in the hospital now. Daddy says she hasn't woke up and I'm afraid she'll die. And it's all my fault."

Stephanie used a napkin to wipe the tears from Lonnie's sad little face. "No, honey, it was not your fault. It was just an accident. Your parents would never think this was your fault. Here, drink a little of your orange juice while I tell you a story."

" A long time ago when I was a baby, my mother became very sick and a few months later, she died. Since I was just a small baby then, I didn't know what had happened, but later when I got older, I began to think it was my fault that she died. If she had not had me, she would still be alive and my daddy wouldn't be so lonesome."

"I worried about it for a long time and became so sad that I couldn't eat or sleep or play with my friends. When my daddy realized why I was so unhappy, he explained that my being born had nothing to do with my mother's sickness. It was just something that happened, just like your mother's accident. Maybe, you should have listened to your mother and gone to check on Betsy, but the accident could have happened anyway. Sometimes bad things happen that we have no control over. Just be happy you were there to get help for your mother."

Lonnie scrubbed his hands across his eyes. "Are you sure that it wasn't my fault, Miss Boudreau? Would it be okay to tell Daddy what happened?"

"I am absolutely and positively sure it was not your fault. And yes, you should talk with your daddy. Now let's go and tell Mrs. Abbot you won't have to visit her anymore." Stephanie wanted the counselor to call Mr. Spalding and prepare him for Lonnie's confession.

Stephanie and Lonnie walked down the hall to Mrs. Abbot's office hand in hand. Suddenly, she became aware of her very wet blouse and smiled. No problem, Maggie would bring her another one to wear for the rest of the school day.

Chapter 15

Stephanie loved teaching but her job would only last a few more weeks. The Country Day alumni dance was looming ahead and she still didn't have an escort. She remembered who Ginger had suggested she should invite and thought, *why not?* She had enjoyed the boat trip and the times they had been out together. Michael was fun to be with and so gorgeous he would make her girlfriends drool with envy.

That evening at dinner, Boudreau excused himself from the table and left Stephanie and Michael alone to finish their coffee and dessert. Stephanie's eyes followed her father as he left the room. "Does Daddy look a bit pale to you?" she asked. "He doesn't usually turn down Maggie's peach pie."

Aware of the senator's illness, Michael didn't know how to answer, so he shook his head and changed the subject, "Since school will be out soon, what are your plans for the rest of the summer?" He could see the worry in her lovely hazel eyes, but it was not his place to tell her the senator's secret.

Stephanie drew her eyes away from the door and looked at Michael. He was wearing a green and white striped dress shirt. He had taken off his coat and tie and hung them on the hat tree in the foyer. The green color in his shirt seemed to turn his eyes green under the lights of the chandelier. A curl of dark hair had fallen across his forehead, giving him a rakish look. At his throat where he had loosened the first button of his shirt, a few curly dark chest hairs had escaped. Stephanie had the strange impulse to reach across and touch the hairs to see how they felt. Were they crisp or were they soft to the touch?

The tap of Maggie's heels as she came through the swinging door to begin clearing the table pulled Stephanie's eyes away from Michael. Attuned to Stephanie's every mood, Maggie gave Stephanie a long look, picked up the dishes and went back to the kitchen.

Stephanie glanced back at Michael and answered his question. "I'm not sure, but there is the big dance at the Oglethorpe Club soon. I was…um, wondering if you would like to be my escort?" She gave him a half-smile and dropped her long dark lashes, unaware of the beguiling picture of southern sweet innocence she made.

Michael was delighted to be invited. This was the opportunity he was hoping for, a chance to get really close to her. He almost felt guilty taking advantage—but not quite.

"I can't believe it. A beautiful girl like you doesn't already have a date? What is wrong with these Savannah men? It would be an honor to take you to the dance. Tell me more about it. Should I wear a tux?"

"A tux would be nice but not necessary. I have to tell you, the girls insisted that I ask you. They're all dying to meet you."

The next day, after work, Michael strolled down Drayton

Street toward Pinkie's Lounge. It was a warm spring evening and Michael dodged the one-way traffic across the street to the bar. Michael found he liked walking the historic district whenever he had a chance. He thought less and less of what happened in Las Vegas and was beginning to feel comfortable in Savannah. He enjoyed strolling through the squares and the hustle and bustle of Broughton Street. The historic houses reminded him of old ladies dressed up in shabby clothing. He began to notice and appreciate the beauty of the flowers in the squares and the majestic live oaks with their long gray beard-like moss swinging in the breeze. Even the sharp tang of the dark water of the Savannah River was intriguing.

It was easy to forget his problems during the day when he was busy, but many nights, he couldn't sleep and came downstairs from his apartment to walk in the senator's garden. He would sit on the base of the statue of Aphrodite to smoke a cigarette or drink a beer and find himself talking to the statue.

"What will I do if they send someone after me?" he wondered aloud. "The senator said he will protect me, but how do I know what will satisfy Big Duke? I wish you had some answers for me, Beautiful." Sometimes, it seemed to Michael the statue was actually listening.

By the time Michael reached Pinkie's, the Drayton Street bar was filled with the usual after-work crowd. It was Friday and the customers were looking forward to the weekend. Married men stopped by to relax with a drink before driving home to the wife and children. Single guys and gals congregated, hoping to get lucky. Sometimes money exchanged hands—gambling debts? drugs? Nobody paid attention. People were there to relax and minded their own business.

The bar stools were occupied but Michael spotted an empty booth in the back. When the waitress came by, he ordered a Scotch and waited for Pinkie to spot him.

Pinkie's sharp eyes noticed Michael immediately, but didn't acknowledge him right away. He continued to talk with the regulars at the bar, smiling around the cigarette that dangled from his mouth. He knew where Michael was staying because the senator had told him, but he also realized there was more to the story. Pinkie didn't ask; he wasn't the type to pry. When Michael was ready, Pinkie knew he would tell him.

After a few minutes, Pinkie made his way to the back booth and greeted Michael with a handshake. "How's it going, Michael?"

"Not too bad, Nono," he answered, using the Greek word for godfather. "I'm sorry I haven't been by before now, but lots of things have happened."

As soon as Pinkie slipped into the other side of the booth, the waitress brought him a Coke. "Oh, I've been keeping up. I know where you're staying, since the senator comes in pretty regular and Savannah is still a small town when it comes to gossip. Sooner or later, I hear what's going on. I also know you are working at the DeSoto, and from what Pinkney tells me, you're doing a good job. But, what's all this about you and the senator's daughter?"

Michael ran his hand through his hair, "It's very complicated but I want to tell you about it. Maybe you can give me some advice." He began with the trouble in Las

Vegas and then explained about Senator Boudreau's illness and what the senator had proposed to him.

Pinkie listened quietly while Michael talked continuously for thirty minutes. It felt good to unburden his problems, especially to a sympathetic ear. When he finished, Michael felt wrung out. He caught the waitress' eye and ordered another Scotch. When she brought his drink, she brought Pinkie another Coke. Coca-Cola was Pinkie's choice of drink since childhood because his father worked for the local Coca-Cola bottling company. When there was nothing else to drink in the house, there was always Coke.

Pinkie shook his head. "Sorry about the senator. I noticed he wasn't looking well lately. As for being afraid that someone will come after you from Las Vegas, that's a possibility. I can help you by mentioning it to my policemen friends. They'll keep a lookout for you. On my end, I'll check out all the newcomers carefully. Sooner or later, all visitors come to Pinkie's. As for the deal you made with the senator about his daughter," Pinkie shook his head. "Better think carefully about that. Marriage is a serious step. How do you feel about the girl?"

"I like her. She's a great girl." Giving Pinkie a mischievous look, he continued, "And she's beautiful. There's no downside there, but I don't want to mess up her life. Or mine, for that matter. But, the money is such a temptation. I really need it, Pinkie. It would mean a new start for me. Maybe then my father wouldn't think I'm just a bum."

Pinkie leaned across the table and put his hand on Michael's, his eyes warm with understanding. *So, this is what it's all about,* he thought. He looked at Michael eye to eye

"Is this why you are doing this? To get money to show

your father you're a big man? I know Gus is stubborn and was disappointed when you wouldn't follow in his footsteps in the restaurant business, but you must know he loves you. You're not a teenager any more but a grown man who must take responsibility for his actions. I remember when you were a little boy and came to Savannah to visit. You and your father had such a good time, taking out the boat and fishing. You hung on his every word. What happened?"

Michael looked down at the table, and then up at Pinkie's concerned face. "I really don't know. When I grew older, I was interested in sports and Dad wanted me to help in the restaurant. He always bragged on Dean—how smart he was, how much he helped at the store. I guess I felt left out. The more he bragged on my older brother, the more I did things to annoy him. Now that I look back on it, I was a pretty snotty kid. My poor mother was always in the middle, trying to referee. It wasn't fair to her, I suppose."

"Maybe you should call your mother and tell her where you are. She and Gus must be very worried."

"No, not yet. Not until this Vegas situation is settled one way or the other. I know I can trust you to keep it to yourself. Thanks for listening, Nono."

As Michael slipped out of the booth, he leaned down, put his arms around Pinkie's narrow shoulders and gave him a quick hug. "I'll see you again soon."

Pinkie's eyes were moist as he lit another cigarette and watched his godson walk out the door. A few minutes later, he went to the telephone and dialed a Chicago number.

Chapter 16

Anna climbed the stairs to Gus' home office where her husband did most of his work since Deno took over the management of both restaurants. "I don't want to hang over the boy's shoulder," he had said to Anna. "I still do a lot of the ordering and keep an eye on the books, but Deno is doing fine. Don't want him to think I'm checking up on him."

Gus wanted his office to be strictly utilitarian. "No fancy doo-dads for me," he told Anna when she tried to hang curtains at the double window that let in the morning sun or put up colorful pictures on the wall. Aside from his desk and chair, the only pieces of furniture in the room were two visitor's chairs, a small table that held a coffee pot and a few cups, and a large bookcase behind his desk. Books and files were stacked on the shelves in a haphazard manner, along with a few pictures of the family. Eventually, Gus allowed Anna to hang up some framed photos of the Greek Islands that he had taken himself. He grumbled about it, but after a while he admitted he enjoyed looking at them.

Anna stood at the open door for a few minutes, looking at her husband of thirty-six years, the father of her children, and still the love of her life. His curly black hair was now peppered with gray and the strong, handsome body had thickened a bit, but when he looked at her with that special smile, her heart still fluttered.

She remembered how the girls in the Greek village were green with jealousy when she caught the attention of the tall, dark-eyed visiting 'Americano.' All the villagers assumed he came home to choose a wife. Believing that all Americans were rich, they had no idea how hard he had to work to make a good living or how much he had missed his family in Greece.

When Gus had walked into the village square, he noticed Anna immediately. Taller than most of the other girls, she stood out like a bright sunbeam with her long blond hair and striking blue eyes. He watched her—so slim and graceful—as she danced a spirited folk dance with the other girls. *Yes, she's the one*, he decided.

Anna didn't care about money or the fact that she would have to leave her family. When they were introduced, his dark eyes, as black as Kalamata olives, seemed to reach into her very soul and she was lost.

Gus felt Anna's presence and looked up from his desk to see her standing in the doorway, gazing at him with love in her eyes. He returned her smile and realized he had suddenly grown hard. He wasn't sure if he should be proud or embarrassed. Was this normal for a 67-year-old married man? But to him, Anna was still as beautiful and desirable as the eighteen-year-old he fell in love with at first sight.

"I have wonderful news," said Anna, wearing a big smile on her pretty face, as she hurried into Gus's office. "Pinkie called from Savannah. Michael is there."

"God be praised," said Gus, crossing himself. He got up from his chair to give Anna a hug. "Let's call him, or better still, why don't we go down to Savannah for a visit? I know you've heard from Michael from time to time, but we haven't seen that boy for seven years. Maybe time has knocked some sense into his hard head."

Anna pulled back and took both his hands. "No, Gus. Pinkie said we shouldn't come now. And what you just said is the reason we should not. You have to let Michael find his own way. You saw what happened when you tried to push him into the restaurant business. He's not like Deno. He's like you. He's beautiful and has a good heart, but stubborn. Pinkie assured me that Michael's okay. He has a job and has met some nice people who have befriended him. He even has a girlfriend. If we go down there, he may take off again. Pinkie will look out for him and let us know when it's time to go to Savannah."

Gus turned away from Anna and sat back down behind his desk. He put his head in his hands. "You're saying I'm the reason he left?"

"Maybe we're both at fault. I spoiled him and you compared him to Deno. Insisting that Michael work in the restaurant was certainly why he left Chicago. I know you love him, but you are too much alike, both head strong and want your own way. He's a grown man. You couldn't tell him what to do when he was a teenager, and you certainly can't now. Why don't we leave him alone for the time being? I'm just grateful to know that he is all right and that Pinkie is there for him."

"Yes, of course you're right. Pinkie is close as family. He always took time with Michael when we visited Tybee Beach when the kids were small. He told me once he wished he had a son like Michael. He'll be there for him if he needs anything." Gus loved Pinkie but couldn't help but resent that Michael would go to him instead of coming home. Gus would wait but he wouldn't wait for long.

Anna walked behind Gus and put her arms around his neck and kissed the top of his head. Giving him a cocky smile, she whispered in his ear, "Maybe this girl will straighten him out. Look how well I straightened out your life."

"Straightened out my life?" He laughed. "More like tangled it up. But I loved every minute of it." In a quick move, he swiveled his chair around, took hold of her waist, and set her on his knees. "Let's see who straightens out who." And he gave her a big kiss.

Chapter 17

In preparation for the dance, Michael rented a tux, ordered a wrist corsage, and made a visit to Levy Jewelers on Broughton Street. In the evening, when he arrived at the senator's mansion to pick up Stephanie, Maggie let him in with her usual dour look.

"Do I pass inspection?" he asked, making a complete turn.

Maggie rolled her eyes. "Well, pretty is what pretty does, my mama always says," and she walked into the kitchen and slammed the door.

Michael shook his head as a soft laugh drifted down from the staircase. He glanced up as Stephanie floated down, a vision in deep rose. Her dress fell like a slim column down to the tips of her high heel sandals. The front of the dress was draped leaving her arms bare and the back almost non-existent. Diamonds sparkled at her neck and dripped from her ears. Her shoes were transparent as glass, showcasing manicured toes the color that matched the dress.

"Wow, you're the classiest Cinderella I've ever seen. You look sensational." *Being married to her wouldn't be bad at all*, he thought to himself as he handed Stephanie the corsage.

"It really bugs you that Maggie doesn't like you, doesn't it?" she said as she smiled and slipped the flowers on her wrist. "Good to know at least one woman is impervious to your charm."

"Does that mean that you find me charming?" he teased, kissing her hand and running his thumb on the inside of her palm.

"Not sure yet, still trying to figure that one out," she shrugged as she picked up a chiffon stole, a shade deeper than her dress, threw it over her arm and floated out the front door.

The dance was held at the Oglethorpe Club on Gaston Street in Savannah's Historic District. The stately mansion was originally built in 1857 as a private residence by Edmund Molyneux and has been the home of the Oglethorpe Club since 1870, the oldest and most prestigious gentlemen's club in Georgia.

Earlier that day when Peaches heard that Stephanie had invited Michael to the Oglethorpe Club, she rolled her green eyes, a shade deeper green in envy. "My, my," she snickered, "You're stepping in high cotton. Pretty fancy for a Greek guy, new to Savannah, and from Chicago, too." Michael returned her look with a killer smile. He would never admit he was a little nervous about mixing with her fancy friends. At the same time, he was looking forward to spending more time with Stephanie.

When Stephanie introduced Michael to her friends at the dance, everyone was very polite to him. Secretly, the women checked out his sexy looks while the men wondered who the hell he was.

"You must be crazy, girl," Ginger whispered to Stephanie, "I'd have jumped him the first time I saw him. He's gorgeous. A real Greek god."

Dancing began after dinner. While Stephanie danced with another man from their table, Michael asked Ginger to dance.

"Listen, Sugar," she drawled. "Don't know what's going on between you and Steff, and I don't poach on my best friend, but if things don't work out, give me a call. I promise you the best time of your life."

She rubbed against him to punctuate the invitation. Ginger was the most blatant, but some of the other women made it clear they were more than just interested.

Stephanie was pleased to find that Michael was a good dancer. Their bodies fit well since she was only a couple of inches shorter in her heels. He held her close for the slow dances, kissed her hair and ran his hands down her bare back. She could feel his arousal and couldn't help but wonder if they would fit as well in other, more intimate ways. She immediately shook her head to dislodge the erotic thought.

Michael felt the movement and pulled back, "Is there something wrong? I love holding you like this, but how much longer do we have to stay?"

She looked up into those passionate turquoise eyes and made a decision. "Let's go now," she whispered.

Nothing was said on the ride home. As soon as they got inside the house and shut the door, they turned to each other in a hot, desperate embrace, lips and tongues meeting and exploring. Michael had been thinking all evening that Stephanie was wearing nothing under that spectacular dress and he made his move to find out. He slipped the dress off her shoulder, following with kisses down to the swell of her breast.

Stephanie's breath was coming in short gasps. "No, not here. Come upstairs. Daddy sleeps like a log and Maggie's room is in another wing."

Michael didn't argue but followed her up the stairs into a large bedroom. He had impressions of a beautifully decorated feminine room, but his mind was elsewhere as he led her to the large bed and whisked off her dress in one quick swoop. He was right; all she had on was a lacy black triangle. She was slim but well proportioned with small high breasts and long slender legs.

As soon as he took off his jacket, Stephanie began to unbutton his shirt. "Too slow," he said and quickly stripped off his shirt and pants. He was down to his shorts, when he remembered what was in his pocket. Michael willed himself to slow down and get in control. This was more than a one night stand for him. He had long-range plans.

Taking a little box out of the pocket of the coat he had slung to the floor, he sat on the bed next to Stephanie and took her in his arms.

"Stephanie, I have a gift for you. It's not much but I want you to know that I have become very fond of you. I want you very much, but my feelings for you are more than just physical."

He opened the box and took out a little gold ring with a Greek key design. "Let's call it a prelude to something more permanent. Let me put it on your finger."

On the verge of surrender, Stephanie's hazel eyes turned cold. "You must be out of your mind. Do you think I haven't suspected what you and Daddy are cooking up? I don't need another man to tell me how to run my life. I'll sleep with you because I want to, but if you think there's going to be a 'happily ever after' ending to this relationship, you can go right back to Vegas."

Michael was furious; all romantic thoughts vanished. "I don't need someone just to have sex with. I can have any woman I want. I thought we had something more going here. But I guess I was wrong. You can go to hell."

He hurriedly dressed and ran down the stairs. On the way out of the house, he spotted a bottle of brandy on the dining room sideboard. Grabbing it, he bolted out the side door. He didn't notice Maggie standing in the dark kitchen doorway holding a glass of water.

"Oh, no," she mumbled. "That sorry piece of trash was up in Steffie's room. I gotta do somethin'."

Chapter 18

Once in the garden, Michael went straight to the statue of Aphrodite and sat at the base. Since Stephanie rejected him, it was obvious he had to leave Savannah. Where could he go to hide? He opened the bottle of brandy and took a long deep swallow, then another.

"Well, Aphrodite, looks like it's just me and you. I bet you wouldn't refuse my ring." Yes, it was still in his pocket. "Let's see if it fits your finger." He slipped the ring onto the marble finger of the statue. "How 'bout that? Fits perfectly."

He continued to drink from the bottle as he tried to formulate a plan. Should he speak to Pinkie and ask advice or go back home and face his father? No. Either way, it would be too humiliating. He had some friends in New Orleans. That might be a good place to hide. His eyelids grew heavy and he slept.

My God, what a dream! Michael didn't know where he was but it seemed he was floating on a cloud. Next to him was a beautiful woman. She was naked, with long blond hair, eyes the color of the summer sky, and full, sensuous lips. And what a body! It was pale as Italian marble, lush breasts, narrow waist and full rounded hips. On her finger was a slim gold ring. Her long legs were wrapped around him, her mouth hot on his. She was insatiable. She wanted him again and again. He didn't have to hold back. It was just a dream.

Michael awoke just before dawn, lying naked at the base of the statue of Aphrodite. Next to him was an empty bottle of brandy. No wonder his head was pounding and his body felt sore. He pulled on his wrinkled clothes and started to leave when he looked up and saw the ring on the statue's finger.

"God, I must have been really wasted last night."

He shook his head to clear it, but that made it hurt even more. He reached up to remove the ring from the statue's finger, but the ring wouldn't come off. He twisted it and pulled it, but it was stuck. "Let it go, you bitch."

"No, you belong to me now."

What? Did the statue say something? No, he must bearing things. I'll never drink that much again, he promised himself. Wrapping one arm around the statue, and placing his other hand around the ring, he tugged as hard as he could, but the ring would not come off the marble finger.

A light came on in the kitchen. *Maggie must already be up and starting breakfast. Oh my God!* She mustn't see him. Michael grabbed his jacket and ran up the stairs to his apartment.

There was no way he could go to work today so he called in sick. "No problem," said Phillip. "Looks like a slow day. Just take care of that sore throat. Peaches and I will handle everything."

Michael crawled into bed and tried to get some sleep, but it was impossible. His mind kept replaying the erotic dream with the woman. *God, she looked just like the statue of Aphrodite. It was a dream, wasn't it? Then there was the ring. Did I give I to her? I must be losing my mind.*

As soon as he thought Pinkie would be at the bar, Michael pulled on jeans, a t-shirt, and slipped on his tennis shoes. He quietly sneaked down the stairs and drove to town, parking his car on a side street. When he walked into Pinkie's Bar, he was glad to see it was almost empty.

"Well, look who's here," said Pinkie when Michael came in. "Glad to see you again so soon, but, you don't look so good. How about a brew on the house? Maybe that'll cheer you up and put some color in your face."

"Thanks, Pinkie, but I'd rather have coffee." Michael sat on one of the stools at the bar. He was tired and confused and needed to confide in someone he trusted. He lit a cigarette and gazed around the walls, at the pictures of politicians and celebrities, all of them Pinkie's friends, and tried to decide how to explain what had happened, when he didn't even understand it himself.

Michael put out his cigarette and looked at Pinkie. "I don't know if you can help me, but I need some advice. You were always there for me when I was a kid and my family visited Savannah. I could talk to you when I couldn't talk to my father."

Pinkie poured a cup of coffee and set it in front of Michael. "What's going on? You know you can trust me. Is it about the senator and his daughter or have you heard something from Vegas?"

"Pinkie, I know you'll think I'm crazy. And maybe I am." He ran his hands through his hair and took a deep breath.

"There's a statue in the garden at the senator's house. Last night, I had too much to drink and I dreamed that I had… uh…well, that the statue and I…uh…Oh, God," Michael put his head down, unable to look Pinkie in the face.

"But, it was so real. I swear it really happened. I put a ring on the statue's finger but she wouldn't let me take it off. Then, she spoke to me. I know you won't believe it, but I think it really happened." Not able to continue, he shook his head and rubbed his red-rimmed eyes.

Pinkie's eyes grew large, and for a few seconds, he was speechless. Then, he laughed and patted Michael on the shoulder. "Boy, I've heard some really wild stories after a drunken night, but yours takes the cake. You must've had way too much to drink and were hallucinating. Don't you know it's dangerous to drink that much? It can ruin your health."

"You haven't been talking to the guys on the street, the ones who tell stories about the Savannah ghosts, have you? There's all kind of ghost stories about this town. Some folks even claim their house is haunted, but I never believed in all that stuff. Forget the coffee. Maybe you need a stiff drink. You know what they say about the hair of the dog, don't you?"

Michael felt sick and just shook his head.

Chapter 19

"You're up early this morning," said Maggie handing Stephanie a cup of coffee when she came into the kitchen. "I s'pected you to sleep late after the big dance last night. Didn't hear you come in."

"Thanks, Maggie. I want to talk to Daddy before he gets away this morning." Stephanie sat down at the table and sipped her coffee.

Maggie sat down across from Stephanie and looked straight into her eyes. "Look here, Baby, I should have told you before. Your daddy's sick, real sick. You need to stop your foolishness and take care of him."

Stephanie's face turned ashen with shock. Her hand shook as she set down her cup. "What are you saying? There's nothing wrong with Daddy."

"Well, there is. He's got cancer and he's afraid to tell you. I know you love him even though you don't act like it sometimes. Y'all only have each other."

Before Stephanie could answer, Boudreau came into the kitchen. "Good morning, sweetheart. How was the dance last night?" Walking behind his daughter's chair, he kissed the top of her head.

"It was okay, but that's not important. Daddy, please sit down, I want to talk to you." Hearing the concern in his daughter's voice, the senator looked at Maggie and she nodded.

Boudreau sat down at the table and sighed. "I guess the cat's out of the bag. I just didn't want to worry you." He reached across and took her hand. "I didn't want to make you sick again."

"Daddy, you are the most important person in my life. If you don't know that, it's my fault. I've been very selfish, wallowing in my misery when you needed me. I want to hear what the doctors have to say. In fact, I want to go with you to your next appointment. Have your doctors said anything about going to Duke? They do wonders these days. We Boudreaus are fighters. We don't give up." Stephanie got up from the table and put her arms around her father.

"Thank you, Jesus," whispered Maggie.

Chapter 20

Maggie's Story

M aggie came to Savannah with Stephanie's mother, when Amanda Simpson left Charleston to marry Winston Boudreau. Only eighteen, Maggie had fallen in love with a merchant seaman in Charleston, who dazzled her with his charm and good looks, got her pregnant, and disappeared with his ship when she told him he was to be a father. The baby was born prematurely and was too small to survive.

Crushed with the double disappointment, Maggie welcomed the opportunity to leave heartbreak behind and move to Savannah and work for the Boudreaus. A year later, Amanda gave birth to a baby girl and Maggie took over the care of baby Stephanie. Amanda, a lovely but delicate Southern beauty, never completely regained her health after the difficult birth. When Stephanie was six month old, Amanda developed a particularly vicious strain of pneumonia and died at the age of twenty-two.

For months, Boudreau was prostrate with grief. When he was finally able to manage his sorrow, he transferred his love to his baby daughter. Although he had woman friends through the years, and sometimes lovers, he never remarried. Maggie stayed on and since Stephanie was too young to remember Amanda, Maggie was the only mother she ever knew. Both the senator and Stephanie considered her a member of the family.

Over the years, Maggie dated a few men but only one seriously. He asked her to marry him, but that meant moving to Atlanta and she would not leave Stephanie and the senator, since she considered them her family, as well.

Maggie's role was now house manager and cook. She supervised the women who came in to clean the mansion and wash and iron clothes, and she kept an eye on José, the gardener. The senator had not asked her to watch José, but she kept an eye on him anyway.

Maggie made her own schedule to accommodate the senator and Stephanie. She cooked dinner each night except on weekends. She made breakfast when the senator or Stephanie was at home, and on Sunday, she provided a midday meal. Maggie was free to leave the house whenever she was not needed, but always let the senator know where she was going.

Since the day was fine, and the senator and Stephanie needed to be alone, Maggie climbed into her old Chevy for a visit to her mother who lived sixty miles away in the South Carolina low country. The senator told her more than once he would help her buy another car if she needed money. Maggie could afford a newer car on her salary, but she was comfortable with the old one. She had even given the car a name. She called it Susie. She didn't know why she picked that name; it just seemed to fit.

Maggie drove into town and went over the Talmadge Bridge

that spanned the Savannah River and separated Georgia from South Carolina. Taking a right off U.S. Highway 17 toward Hilton Head Island onto a narrow two-lane road, she made several turns and crossed two small bridges that brought her to the edge of a swampy area and her mother's cabin. When she drove up Maggie wished, and not for the first time, that her mother didn't live in such an isolated place.

Mama Sally had spent most of her adult life in Charleston, working as a housekeeper in one of the downtown hotels. She retired five years ago and moved back to the cabin where she was born in the Carolina low country and lived with her mother, Granny Ulla, until Granny's death last year.

Years ago, there had been several Gullah families living in that area. Now, Mama Sally's cabin was one of only two left. George, an elderly man, occupied the other cabin. The rest of the folks had died or moved to towns and cities for school or work and never returned.

Back in her youth, Granny Ulla had been well known in the Gullah community. She was a healer, highly respected for her knowledge of herbs and potions. She delivered most of the babies in the village and some said she had second sight. Maggie remembered her grandmother well and loved the stories she used to tell. Sally always played down her mother's occult accomplishments but agreed that she "knew her medicine plants."

Maggie found her mother on the porch sitting in a rocking chair weaving sweet grass into a basket. Sally braided beautiful baskets with unusual and intricate designs. Her baskets were well made and were among the first to be purchased at the marketplace in Charleston.

Maggie marveled how pretty her mother was. She had grown late into her beauty, having been too tall, too thin and awkward in her youth. Today, she was dressed in a flowing dress of red, green, and yellow, with her snow white hair tied up in a turban to match the dress. Her black eyes were sharp and clear. She stood up and brushed the rushes off her skirt and gave Maggie a strong hug when her daughter walked up the porch steps

"Good to see you, my girl. I was hopin' you'd come today. I made some of Granny's soup to share with you. But what's wrong?" Sally asked when she pulled back and looked at Maggie's unsmiling face.

"Oh, Mama. It's all so sad. I had to tell Steffie about the senator's cancer. She's so broke up about it. I hated to leave her but I thought she and her daddy should have some time alone." Maggie's eyes glistened with unshed tears as she pulled up a second rocker and sat down.

"Jes' sit there and I'll bring you a cup of tea." Sally went into her small kitchen where the kettle was already steaming. She poured the hot water over a mixture she blended herself and added a bit of moonshine, because it seemed to her that Maggie needed it. She poured another cup, without the extra ingredient, and brought both cups out to the porch. "Here, honey, this will make you feel better."

"Thank you, Mama. You always know what I need. Who-eee," she said as she sipped the tea. "I see you put some of your famous home brew in it. Good thing I brought my pajamas. I won't be able to drive back this evenin'." She smiled and took another sip.

"It's good to see you smile, honey. I know how much you

love Stephanie. You couldn't love her more if she wuz your own flesh and blood. You gave all the love to Stephanie that you had for that poor li'l baby you lost. And, I know she love you, too. But, she's a grown woman and you and the senator still treat her like a baby. It's her turn to take care of him, now."

"It's not only the senator's sickness, Mama. It's that good for nothing Michael and his charming handsome self. I saw him sneaking down from Steffie's room last night. He's going to break my baby's heart. I just know he is."

"Oh, I see, you think jus' cause he's good-lookin' like somebody you usta know long time ago, you 'spect him to be the same. You don't know how he feel, Maggie. Why don't you talk to him, ask him? You raised that girl. She ain't got no mama 'cept for you. You gotta right."

"I know, Mama, but there's something more. I told you before 'bout that evil statue in the garden. Michael's always going to that statue and talking to it and putting his hands on it. I know it's haunted and it's put a spell on him. I'm sure the statue turned around the other day and I swear it has a smile on its face. I asked José about it but he didn't know what I was talking about. I told the senator, too, but he laughed and said I was imagining things. I wish Granny was still alive so she could come up with a spell or something to use against it. I'm afraid that statue is gonna hurt Steffie in some way."

"Now, Maggie, you goin' too far. I know Granny filled your head with all that Gullah magic nonsense when you wuz little, but I never had any faith in it. She was a good woman who knew her medicine and helped people, but she didn't have no strange powers. And I don't b'lieve the statue in the senator's garden is haunted either. Now, let's talk about something else. I want to enjoy havin' you here the rest of the day."

"Okay, Mama, but I want to say one more thing." She reached under her blouse and pulled out the *wanga* bag she wore on a ribbon around her neck. "Granny gave me this to protect me and I always wear it. It makes me feel safe. But I wish I had one for Steffie. Don't you have some of Granny's things? Do you suppose there's another *wanga* bag in her stuff?"

"I don't think so, honey, but I'll look if it make you feel better."

"Thank you, Mama. I won't say no more 'bout what's going on in Savannah. Now, tell me what you've been doin'. Have you been to Chas'ton to visit your sisters?"

Maggie changed the subject and the rest of the day passed pleasantly with talk of family and gumbo soup. But, in the back of Maggie's mind, lurked the statue of Aphrodite.

Chapter 21

When Maggie returned to the Boudreau mansion the next morning, Stephanie had taken over her kitchen. She had already made coffee and was getting ready to break eggs in a bowl.

"Good heavens, child. It's been a long time since I saw you wearing an apron in my kitchen." She remembered a much younger Stephanie making cookies with cookie dough all over the counter and even some on her nose.

"Well, you weren't here and I wanted to be sure Daddy ate a good breakfast. As for the apron, I didn't want to get my dress splattered since I'm going to the doctor's office with Daddy later this morning."

Maggie noticed the dark circles under Stephanie's eyes. "Let me have that apron, honey, and you sit down and have some coffee. I'm here, now. I know you didn't sleep much last night. I want to say I'm sorry I didn't tell you 'bout your daddy's sickness but he made me promise I wouldn't tell."

"I'm not mad with you, Maggie, I know you love us both and you did what you had to do, but honestly, it was foolish for Daddy to keep this from me. I'm not a child to be protected. I'm making it my business to learn everything I can about his cancer and see to it that he gets the best possible care. I am not losing him, not for a long, long time." Stephanie's voice thickened at the last words as she sat down at the table and wiped the moisture from her eyes with a napkin.

Maggie put her arms around Stephanie's shoulders and pressed her head to her ample bosom. "That goes for me, too, baby. I'll do everything I can to help you make the senator well. Listen, I want to give you something." She reached around her neck and took off the *wanga* bag and put it around Stephanie's neck. "My Granny Ulla made it for me, to keep me safe. I know you don't believe in such things, but please wear it. Please do it, for me."

Stephanie saw the concern and love in Maggie's ebony eyes. "Of course, I will," she said and gave her a kiss on her dusky cheek. "I remember Granny Ulla. She used to send me medicine to drink whenever I was sick. It always tasted nasty, but it did seem to help me get better."

I wonder if I can get Daddy to wear this amulet, thought Stephanie. *He needs it more than I do and it can't hurt.*

Stephanie and the senator left for the doctor's office around mid-morning, telling Maggie that they wouldn't be back for lunch but would see her at dinner time.

Later that day Maggie observed Michael from the kitchen window, as he walked from the drive across the garden toward the carriage house. He was wearing a pair of jeans and a wrinkled t-shirt. Instead of stopping to talk to the statue as usual, Michael put his head down, skirted around the statue and quickly ran up the steps.

"That's strange," Maggie mumbled.

When Michael came into the kitchen an hour later, he

had changed into chinos and a short sleeve shirt. His hair was shower damp and he smelled of soap. "Hi, Maggie, I see the senator's Cadillac is gone but Stephanie's convertible is here. Will you please tell her I'd like to see her?"

Maggie gave him a sharp look, "She's not here. Nobody home but me."

Thinking he would get no more information from Maggie, Michael turned to leave.

"You want a cup of coffee? Got pecan pie, too."

Michael stopped in his tracks, not sure if he had heard correctly. He turned around and looked at Maggie, a surprised look on his face. "Did you just offer me coffee and pie?" he asked.

"Somethin' wrong with your ears? Sit down." Michael sat at the table, not sure what was coming next.

Maggie poured Michael a cup of coffee, remembering that he drank it black. She cut a large wedge of pecan pie and set it in front of him, and added a fork and a napkin. Then she poured a cup of coffee for herself, put in a little milk, and sat down at the table across from him. The whole time, Michael's wary eyes tracked her movements.

"Go ahead and eat. It's not poison," she smiled. It was a nice, wide smile, showing a full mouth of white teeth. "Scared ya', didn't I?"

Michael let out a breath he wasn't aware he was holding. He couldn't help but smile back. He picked up the fork and began eating the most delicious pecan pie he had ever tasted.

"Okay, now, while you're gobblin' up that pie, listen to what I got to say. I love Stephanie like she was my own. I raised her from a baby and she don't know another mother except for me. So, if you are planning on hurting my baby, you're gonna have to climb over me. And that won't be easy. So, I'm warning you now. I don't know you, but you are too slick and too pretty for a girl like her, and she's done been hurt once already. She knows about her daddy's cancer and she's got a heavy load to carry. I don't know what you and the senator are planning but you need to back off now and let her tend to him. You understand what I'm saying?"

"Maggie, I promise you I would never do anything to hurt Stephanie. I respect her and like her too much to cause her any pain. In fact, I want to do everything I can to help her and the senator. He's been very good to me. I'm sorry about the senator's illness, but I think it best that she knows. I hope he hasn't waited too long to tell her. My situation is very complicated so I don't want to go into it right now. I want to stay in Savannah, but it may not be possible for me to be here much longer."

Michael stepped to the window and looked toward the garden. Aphrodite sparkled in the afternoon sun. *Is that a smile on her face? No, that's impossible. Statues can't smile.* Suddenly, the hair on his arms stood up and the room seemed to grow cold. Fighting for control, he turned and went back to the table, rubbing his hands over his arms to warm them.

"Maggie, you've been here a long time. What can you tell me about the statue out in the garden? Where did it come from? Was the statue here when you moved to this house?"

"Yes, it was, and I've always hated it 'cause I know it's evil! But, you have to ask the senator where it came from. We moved here from downtown ten years ago, mostly 'cause the senator wanted to be close to the water so he could have a boat. The senator found the statue somewhere and had it put in the garden right before the house was finished. I told him it's haunted but the senator just laugh at me."

"If I wanted to do some research on the statue, where would I go here in Savannah?"

"I don't rightly know. You have to ask the senator 'bout that, too. I know there's a libbery 'cross from Forsyth Park that has lots of old books and stuff."

Chapter 22

"Hey," said Phillip when Michael walked into the office the next morning. "How do you feel? You still look a little pale. Maybe you should've stayed home another day."

"I'm okay. I didn't get enough sleep yesterday, that's all. How's everything going here? Anything I should know about? How about the dinner for the visiting mayors? Should I talk to the chef about the meal?"

"Everything's under control. Did you think we couldn't get along without you for one day?" Phillip smiled but Michael could see the glint of annoyance in his eyes.

"No, no, man, I know you can get along without me. You did it before I came here. I'm just a little fuzzy this morning. Maybe, I should have stayed home another day."

"Why don't you go in the kitchen and get some coffee to clear your head. The kitchen crew will want to see you, anyway. They heard you were sick when you weren't here yesterday. When you come back to the office, I want to talk to you about something personal."

Michael shook his head as he walked out of the office and downstairs to the kitchen. *What the hell is the matter with me*, he thought. *I need to get my head straight before I mess up the good relationship I have here at work. It's that damn Aphrodite. I've got to figure out how to get rid of that statue.*

After a cup of coffee, a muffin, and the exchange of jokes with the kitchen staff, Michael returned to the catering office. "Here, Phillip, I brought you one of the chef's delicious apple and cinnamon muffins to make up for my comments earlier this morning."

"That's okay, Michael, I should apologize to you. I shouldn't have gotten my back up. I know you didn't mean anything by it. I'm rather distracted myself. I want to talk to you before Peaches gets back from her meeting with Miss McDonald, the girl who is planning a wedding."

"I did notice that Peaches wasn't here. What's the matter? Trouble in paradise? I thought things were going very well between the two of you."

"Well, they are and they aren't. We eat lunch together almost every day and date on the weekends when Peaches is free. Sometimes she goes home for the weekend and I know she dates other guys." Phillip frowned at the thought of Peaches with someone else. "I think she likes me, but I want to move the relationship along...um...so, we can get, you know...um... closer. I thought you could help me."

Michael tried not to smile, but he couldn't help it. "You mean to want to get her in bed."

"Oh, God, yes! I mean, No! I mean yes, eventually." Michael couldn't remember ever seeing a grown man blush before. "But I seem to be stuck at first base. I want to be more than just her best friend. I dated some in college but since then I've had to take care of Mother and haven't had time for a girlfriend. Since Peaches came to work here, I haven't wanted anyone else. She's so beautiful and smart, when you get to know her. I just don't know what to do to get her to think of me as more than just a friend."

"Okay now, let's think about the situation." Michael rubbed his chin, happy to be distracted by Phillip's problem, thus forgetting about his own for a short while.

"Let's see now, she's a gorgeous girl, but everyone must tell her that. You need to approach her in a different way. You say she's smart. So, tell her how much you appreciate her work here in the office. Praise her when she does something particularly well. Find out what her interests are so you can discuss them with her. Show her you like her for what's inside her head, not only for that knock-out body."

"I know she likes decorating. She's always reading magazines about furniture and stuff like that and she likes to go to antique stores. I saw her apartment once. It was beautiful and she told me she picked up all those items from garage sales and second-hand stores."

"Well, there you are." Michal slapped a hand on his desk. "Ask if you can go with her when she hunts for bargains, or ask her to help you purchase something for your house. Become interested in what she's interested in. But, tell me this, have you kissed her yet? I mean really kissed her?"

Phillip's eyes shifted away from Michael. "Uh, well, on the cheek and just a peck on the lips. I get nervous when I get close to her. I don't want to embarrass myself."

"Oh, man, you're afraid to let her know she arouses you." Michael shook his head and smiled. "But, don't you get it? How else is she to know how you feel? Knowing she does that to you will make her feel powerful. Next time you take her home, give her a big sexy kiss and see if she responds. My guess is she will. If not, you apologize and say you just got caught up in the moment. What have you got to lose?"

Just then, the door opened and Peaches breezed in wearing four-inch heels and a clingy green dress. "Hi guys, we got the McDonald wedding. Glad you're back, Michael." She stopped dead when she saw the 'deer in the headlights' expression on Phillip's face. "What's going on here?"

"Uh, nothing," stammered Phillip. "I guess you just startled us. That's wonderful about the McDonald wedding. I didn't think the mother would go for it when I talked to her yesterday. You really turned her around. Good work, Peaches." He dragged his flustered eyes away from her and turned to Michael. "We'll have to let Peaches take over all the weddings from now on. She's great with the mothers."

Peaches smiled with pleasure at the compliment. "Thanks, Phillip. Sometimes it just takes a woman-to-woman talk, especially when it comes to weddings." She didn't say anything else, but Peaches was not fooled. She knew they were talking about her. As Phillip had discovered, she was smart.

At the end of the day, Michael asked Phillip about the old library that Maggie had mentioned. "Oh, you must mean the Georgia Historical Society Library on Gaston and Whitaker streets. Why do you want to know?"

"Just curious about something the senator said about Savannah back during the Civil War. I just want to look it up," Michael lied.

"Okay," Phillip laughed. "But, you better call it The War Between the States or the ladies working at the Historical Society will call you a 'damn Yankee' and pitch you out the door."

Chapter 23

After work that afternoon, Michael ran up the steep steps of the Georgia Historical Society Library, a stately building on the corner of Whitaker and Gaston. A woman who couldn't have been taller than five feet was just locking the door. She wore a white long sleeve silk blouse tied in a bow under a pointed chin, a brown mid-calf skirt, and low-heeled pumps. Her fluffy white hair was pulled to a bun on the top of her head. Michael guessed her age to be around 70. She turned penetrating blue eyes, behind rimless spectacles on Michael.

"You're too late, young man. We close at five."

"I'm sorry. I'm new in Savannah and didn't know the library hours. I need help with some research. My name is Michael Andrews." He gave her his well-practiced 'little boy lost' smile, that usually melted older women.

"Hmm. And what is it you want to research, young man?" she asked in her soft Southern voice.

"An old statue of Aphrodite, the Greek goddess. It's in a garden here in Savannah. I want to find out where it came from."

Even though Michael's height made it impossible, she

somehow managed to look down at him from her patrician nose. "It would seem to me that the best way to find that out is to ask the person who owns the statue."

"There are reasons why I can't do that right now." Frustration showing in his face, he added, "Can you please help me?"

"Well, young Michael Andrews. I always like a mystery. That's why I volunteer here. My name is Emily Habersham and we are open from nine a.m. to five p.m. except on Sunday. When can you come?"

Michael's face lit up. "Thank you. I can come on my lunch break, about noon each day. Let me help you down the steps and into your car, Mrs. Habersham."

She gave him a smile that revealed the beauty she had once been. "Oh, thank you, I can go down these steps by myself just fine, but I never turn down the assistance of a good looking man," she drawled as she took his offered arm.

That evening when Michael arrived at his apartment, he called Stephanie on her private line. After what had happened in her room after the dance, he was afraid she wouldn't want to speak to him, so when she answered, he immediately blurted out, "Stephanie, don't hang up. I called to apologize for the other night. Please say you'll forgive me. What I did and what I said was inappropriate. I have more respect for you than any woman I have ever known. Please say you'll give me another chance."

Stephanie's voice sounded as if she had been crying. "Oh, Michael I'm too tired to go into that right now. I'm so upset about Daddy."

"I understand and I wouldn't have called except I feel so bad about what happened that I can't sleep. Can we talk soon, when you're not so tired? Please say we can still be friends."

"I'm not sure what happened that night. I think we both had too much to drink. I said some things that I shouldn't have, also. But, I can't deal with it right now. I can only promise that we will talk and try to clear the air soon."

"I guess I'll have to accept that. Just remember that I care for you and for the senator. Please let me know if there is any way I can help."

"Thank you. I have to go now."

She sounded so vulnerable and weary that it broke Michael's heart. He'd give anything to be able to go over there and take her in his arms. What an idiot he had been the other night.

For the next week, Michael spent his lunch hour with Mrs. Habersham at the Georgia Historical Society Library. Together they looked in the card catalog, pored over the pictures in the vertical file, and searched in many reference books on Savannah history. Mrs. Habersham called the head of the History Department at Armstrong College and the librarian at the University of Georgia for information about the Grecian marble statue. Although Michael learned about the famous Savannah Bird Girl statue by Sylvia Shaw Judson and Gracie, the statue of a child that supposedly haunted Bonaventure Cemetery, nothing could be found about a local marble statue of Aphrodite.

"Don't be discouraged, Michael," said Mrs. Habersham.

"I'll continue to look and increase the area of search to the Charleston Historic Society, and even down to Florida."

While Michael was discouraged, Mrs. Habersham face was alight with excitement over the mystery. In her youth, she had been research librarian for the public library and nothing excited her more than poring over musty tomes and reference materials. Besides, she had grown fond of Michael during their hours of research and wanted to find some information about the marble statue to please him.

She could see he was disturbed by the statue even though he wanted to know more about it. In her quiet way she asked, Michael some questions about his background but he was not very forthcoming. Not once did he say to the librarian he thought the statue was haunted. He didn't want to admit that—not even to himself.

Chapter 24

P eaches was covering her typewriter for the day when Phillip walked across the office to her desk. "Are you free to go to the movies this evening? *Cape Fear*, the movie they filmed here in Savannah, is playing at the Lucas. Gregory Peck and Robert Mitchum are in it."

Phillip had been looking for an opportunity to try the new approach with Peaches that Michael had suggested. "We can get a bite to eat first or go to an early show and eat later," he added. He was nervous about becoming more aggressive, but as Michael said, what did he have to lose? *Yeah, just her friendship, that's what.*

Peaches gave him a smile that made his toes curl. "I'd love to see *Cape Fear*. I saw them filming Michum in Forsyth Park when they were shooting the movie." She rolled her eyes. "Mitchum is so sexy. Maybe I'll see myself in the crowd. Let's go to an early movie and eat later so we can take our time. Since it's Friday, we won't have to worry about going to bed early." Just hearing the words, 'going to bed', made Phillip's temperature rise, even though he knew what Peaches meant. The idea of getting into a bed with that gorgeous sexy body turned his mouth dry and scrambled his brain.

The ring of the phone on his desk jerked him back from his fantasy. He stepped back to his desk to answer it, hoping it wasn't a problem that would keep him from leaving the office with Peaches. Peaches was collecting her purse and sweater when she picked up on Phillip's telephone conversation.

"Yes, this is Phillip Hargraves. Oh my God, what happened? Where is she? Yes, I'll be right there."

He placed the phone carefully on the receptacle, his face chalk white. Afraid he was going to faint, Peaches grabbed both his arms and shook him gently.

"What's the matter, Phillip? Talk to me."

"My mother," he managed to say, his voice shaky with fear. "She's been taken to the emergency room at Memorial Hospital. They think she's had a heart attack. I have to go."

"Come, I'll take you. You're in no shape to drive." Peaches took Phillip's hand and led him out of the office.

When Phillip and Peaches went through the sliding glass door of the emergency room of the hospital, a woman wearing a housedress and slippers jumped up from a chair along the wall.

"Phillip," she called. "I brought your mother in a little while ago. I went to your back door to borrow some tea and found her slumped over the kitchen table so I called 911. They won't tell me anything because I'm not a relative. Maybe you can get something out of that closed-mouthed hussy at the desk."

Phillip, too rattled to even thank Mrs. Solomon, went straight to the reception desk. Peaches introduced herself as Phillip's co-worker and thanked the neighbor for calling for help.

"We've been neighbors and friends for a long time," said Mrs. Solomon. "We're always borrowing back and forth and swapping recipes. I'm glad Phillip is here, though. I didn't know what else to do once they brought Annabel here. I was so frightened." She nervously twisted the handkerchief in her hands. "But they did let me ride with her in the ambulance and hold her hand."

Phillip came back from the reception desk, a shade less ashen than before. "They think she's had a mild heart attack and are assessing her condition. Her doctor has been called and is on his way. They feel sure she will have to be admitted." He turned to Mrs. Solomon and gave her a hug.

"Please forgive me for not even speaking to you when I came in. Thank you so much for your quick thinking. The nurses told me what happened. Thank God you went over to the house. I probably would not have come home for several hours. I usually call and let her know if I'll be late, but..." He put his hands over his eyes.

"Now, now, don't start blaming yourself. These things happen. Your mother is always telling me what a good and loving son you are." She rolled her eyes, "I should have a son like you. But, never mind, I need to call mine and have him pick me up. You need to stay here and talk to her doctor when he comes and this pretty young lady needs to stay and take care of you."

"Oh, no, Mrs. Solomon. I'll drive you home, or Peaches will." He looked inquiringly at Peaches, who nodded.

"No , I insist" said Mrs. Solomon. "You both stay here for Annabel. I will call Melvin. He'll grouse, but he'll come. Don't worry about me. I'll go home and pray for my friend.

Just promise you'll let me know how she is." She gave Phillip another hug and smiled at Peaches. "Take care of this boy; he's pretty special." Then she moved away toward the public phones, her slippers slapping against the tile floor.

"I still think we should take her home. Her son is a little rough. He may give her a hard time."

Peaches shook her head. "She impressed me as being a pretty tough lady. I believe she can handle Melvin. Your mom is lucky to have such a great neighbor. Besides, we need to be here for your mother." She took his hand and led him to a chair. "Would you like a cup of coffee or something cold?"

"I don't want anything. God, I am so glad you're here."

"Me, too," she smiled and held on to his hand. There was nothing for them to do but sit and stare at the other people, sitting against the drab green wall of the hospital emergency room, all waiting for word from doctors about their loved ones.

An hour later, Dr. Thurber came out to speak to Phillip and concurred that Annabel had experienced a heart attack but, thank heaven, not a serious one. She had been admitted into the hospital for more tests and observation. In fact, she was already on her way to her room. The doctor suggested Phillip wait a few minutes and then go up and see his mother before she received her sleeping medication. In the morning, after he looked at the results of the tests, he would speak to Phillip again.

"That doesn't sound too bad. I suppose it could be a lot worse," said Phillip to Peaches. Let's go up and see her." More color had returned to his face.

"I'll ride up in the elevator with you, but I don't think

this is the time to meet your mother. Let's wait until she's better and at home before you introduce me. Find out what she needs for you to bring her tomorrow and I'll go home with you and help you pack a small bag for her."

"Gosh, Peaches, I didn't even think of that. Of course, she'll need some personal things, especially if she stays a few days." He rubbed his forehead. "What is wrong with me?"

"Nothing is wrong with you. You're still in shock. Don't worry. By tomorrow morning, you'll be back to your organized, meticulous self again. And, I like that about you."

"You do?" He smiled for the first time since the phone call from the hospital. The elevator door opened just as he was thinking of kissing her. She had been so incredibly sweet and helpful all evening. He couldn't have managed without her.

When he came out of his mother's hospital room a few minutes later, his eyes were shining with suppressed tears. Peaches took his arm as they walked toward the elevator.

"How is she?"

"Very sedated. She's in a white monstrosity of a bed, with the bars pulled up all around her and plugged into several monitors. When I was young, she was a force to deal with and now she looked so small and defenseless. It broke my heart. She could hardly keep her eyes open. I told her that I love her and that she was going to be okay. She gave me a small smile and said 'I love you more,' something we have said to each other since I was small. I squeezed her hand and she fell asleep. I didn't get a chance to ask what she needed for me to bring tomorrow."

Peaches' heart went out to Phillip. *His neighbor was right,* she thought. *He is a special person and so caring of his mother. She couldn't imagine anyone of her seven brothers and sisters having such deep feelings for their parents. Of course, they loved them—they were their parents, for heaven's sake.*

Her mother cooked, cleaned the house, and nursed them when they were sick, but Ma was too tired at the end of the day to tell them she loved them. They just figured she did. And as for Pop, he and the older boys were out in the fields except for meals and bedtime. Maybe there were too many of them in the small farmhouse and they rubbed against each other too much. That's why most of them left the farm for work or more education just as soon as they got their high school diploma.

Although she had a general idea where he lived, Peaches had not been to Phillip's house before. But when he stopped in front of a lovely three story Victorian house, she was impressed. Yes, the house looked as if it needed a coat of paint and the walkway to the front steps was cracked. The roof was patched, but she had seen similar houses in magazines that were worth a lot of money after being remodeled. When Phillip unlocked the front door and she saw the dark, bleak colors on the wall, the worn carpets, and the mix-matched furniture, she wanted to weep. But then she noticed the beautiful curved banister of the staircase going up to the next floor and the crown molding on the ceiling. Peaches began to tingle all over. Boy, wouldn't she love to get her hands on this house and decorate it! A little paint, a lot imagination and, of course, some money, would turn this house into the showplace of the neighborhood.

Phillip saw her mouth drop open when he turned on the

lights and he started to apologize, "I'm sorry the place is so dilapidated. Mother won't allow me to change anything or throw things out. She says they all have happy memories for her." He stopped when she turned and he realized her eyes were wide with amazement.

"Oh no, don't apologize, this house has such good bones. With a reasonable amount of money, it can be a showplace. But, this is not what we came for. Show me your mother's room and let's pack a bag for her."

Phillip led her up the stairs to the master bedroom, a large corner room, with windows facing the street. The double tester bed was covered in a white and rose quilt which looked handmade. Rose drapes hung at the windows and even the walls were painted a pale rose. It looked more like a young girl's room. Peaches didn't hesitate, but went directly to the dresser and found items she thought Mrs. Hargraves would need for a few days. Phillip found a small case in the closet to carry them in.

"I think this is enough for a couple of days," said Peaches. "I hope she won't be in the hospital longer than that, but if she is, we can take her some more things. Why don't you take me home now? We're both tired, and aren't you going to call your sister in New York?"

"Yes, I need to do that. Pamela will want to know about Mother. I doubt if she'll come down, though, especially if Mother's attack is not serious. She only makes it to Savannah once a year."

Phillip's older sister was as an attorney with a high-powered law firm in New York City. Divorce was her specialty. Pamela never really came home after graduating from college and marrying a man from the city. The marriage only survived a couple of years but Pamela got used to the New York style of living and never wanted to come back to Savannah.

Phillip drove the several blocks to Peaches' apartment. He walked her to the door and put his arms around her shoulders.

"Peaches, you have no idea what it meant to have you with me this evening. I don't think I could have managed without you. I can't thank you enough."

"Oh well, that's what friends are for," she said brightly and raised her face to brush her lips across his.

Without thinking, he dropped his hands on either side of her waist and pulled her tight against him. When she opened her mouth in surprise, he slipped in his tongue and let it play lightly against hers. He changed the position of his head for a better fit of lips and did what Michael had suggested. He laid one on her.

For a few seconds, Peaches stiffened. Then, oh my God, she kissed him back. Finally, he backed off and looked at her. Her eyes were half closed and her mouth was wet and slightly swollen. She looked gorgeous. He had almost forgotten about his mother.

"I'm sorry, Peaches, that was inappropriate, especially at this time. But, I'm not sorry I did it," he added with a smile.

'Well," said Peaches, taking a deep breath. "I don't think I'm sorry, either." She turned, went inside and shut the door.

Chapter 25

Monday morning, Peaches came in to work with a smile on her face. Michael was surprised she looked so happy since he knew that Phillip's mother was in the hospital. Phillip had already called in to explain he would be late because he was going to the hospital to talk to his mother's doctor. He also told Michael how much help Peaches had been the night his mother had her heart attack. *Hmm*, thought Michael. *Sounds like something else happened over the weekend.*

"So, I heard about what happened Friday night. Phillip told me he couldn't have managed without you. Said he was a complete basket case, but you were there to see that he kept his head and do what he needed for his mother. I'm glad you were there for him, Peaches. His mother is the only family he has, except for a sister who doesn't seem to be close to them at all."

"I'm glad I was able to help. After all, we've become good friends and Phillip is a real sweet guy. He loves his mother very much and her heart attack almost put him in shock. It's nice to see a man show so much love for his mother. Many kids grow up, leave home and hardly give their parents another thought."

Since last weekend, Peaches had been thinking about her family and was feeling guilty because she didn't visit her mother often enough. If Phillip's mother was okay and he didn't need her this weekend, she planned to go home to Millen.

Michael almost winced at her words. How long had it been since he called his mother? What a sorry son he was compared to Phillip! Yes, the old man could be a bastard, but his mother, his beautiful loving mother, had always understood him. He wanted to call, just to hear her voice, but what could he say? His life was such a mess right now.

"I saw Phil's house for the first time the other night," continued Peaches. "It's a fabulous house on a lovely street, but they've let it run down. I don't think it's a money problem, mostly neglect, because his mother doesn't want anything changed. You know how much I love decorating and remodeling houses. Maybe when Mrs. Hargraves feels better, Phillip can talk to her about letting me give her some ideas. If she doesn't want to change anything inside, the outside could use some work. After all, taking care of an expensive piece of property is an investment."

"You're probably right, Peaches, but I wouldn't bother Phillip about the house right now. Getting his mother well and back home will be his first priority." Michael paused and rubbed his chin. "Look, I don't know how to say this tactfully, so I'm just gonna say it. I don't want you messing with his head right now. You must know he's stupid in love with you. Don't you start liking him because you like his fancy house."

Peaches got up from her desk and poked a long blood-red

fingernail in his chest. She looked up at him from her five feet, three inches, emerald eyes blazing.

"Listen here, Mr. Chicago. Don't you tell me what to do. You had your chance with me and threw it away for that narrow-ass ice princess. That's okay because we wouldn't have rubbed well together anyway. It would've been just flash and burn, and besides, I don't want a man who is prettier than me."

"As for Phillip, I'm not planning to date him just for his goddamn house. I like the guy. I was just talking because I like to decorate houses and his could use some help." She gave him a mischievous grin, "But, I do love his house."

Just as Michael backed away from Peaches, Phillip came in the office door. His hair stood on end as if he had been running his fingers through it and there were dark circles under his eyes from lack of sleep. As soon as he came in, he locked eyes with Peaches. For several seconds, they just looked at each other.

Oh yes. Something more happened Friday night, thought Michael. He tried to hide his smile, but they weren't paying attention to him anyway.

Finally, Phillip turned to Michael. "The news is not too bad. Mother's doctor said she did have a mild heart attack but all her vital signs are good. The doctor thinks she should spend at least one more night at the hospital so the nurses can keep an eye on her for another twenty-four hours, but they'll let her go home tomorrow."

Both Michael and Peaches went up to Phillip. Michael patted him on the back and Peaches gave him a brief hug. "I'm so happy she is going to be okay." she said.

"Peaches, I have to thank you again for all you did last Friday night. I told Mother this morning and she wants to meet you and thank you personally."

"Please stop thanking me, Phillip. I was just doing what any friend would do."

Phillip took her hand and looked into her eyes, "I hope there was more to it than just friendship." Peaches glanced away from Phillip's questioning look and frowned at Michael.

"Uh, excuse me," said Michael. "I have to speak to the kitchen staff about tonight's banquet," and hurriedly left the office.

After Michael closed the door, Peaches answered Phillip, "Yes, I think there was more than just friendship, but Friday night was so intense, with your mother's illness, my concern for you, and then that kiss. My emotions are tangled up right now. Let's just worry about your mother and give us a chance to sort out our feelings. Okay?" She drew her hand away and sat down at her desk. "Now, what can I do to help you make your mother's homecoming more comfortable?"

Phillip tried to hide his disappointment. When she mentioned the kiss, he'd felt his stomach flip and wanted badly just to taste her again. Instead, he said, "Of course, you're right. The problem is that Mother will not be able to go up stairs for a while. I have to figure out where she will sleep. I was thinking of the study, which is next to the parlor. There's an extra bed upstairs I can bring down and the downstairs bath is just next door."

"Yes, I remember that room with the bookshelves. You can move the desk to the side and bring down a small table and lamp for next to the bed. Will she need help during the day when you are at work or do you plan to take time off?"

"I've already spoken to Mr. Pinkney about taking off a couple of days, but after that, I need to make arrangements for her. At this point, I'm not sure how much help she will need. The doctor will tell me tomorrow. I've also thought about asking Mrs. Solomon if she would make lunch for Mother for a while. I can take care of breakfast and dinner."

"Phillip, why don't you go and find Michael. He left so we could have some privacy. If you're going to be out for a couple of days, we need to re-arrange the schedule." She turned in her desk chair and reached for a file.

Phillip sighed. Obviously, Peaches didn't want to talk about their feelings or what happened last Friday night. He had to let it go for now. But, he would bring it up again soon. He was convinced that the heat between them was not one sided. He left the office to look for Michael.

Chapter 26

Michael visited Mrs. Habersham at the Georgia Historical Society that afternoon because he enjoyed her company, and because he was at loose ends since Stephanie and the senator were at Emory Hospital in Atlanta seeing a cancer specialist.

The librarian had increased the area of the search to South Carolina and Florida, but to no avail. She told Michael she had received a phone call from a library in St. Augustine, Florida inquiring if she would like some information about a Greek settlement in that area back in the 1700s, even though there was no mention of a statue.

"Should I ask them to send it?" she asked Michael.

"Sure, there's probably no connection, but ask them to send it anyway. I could use some reading material. Not much else to do in the evenings."

Mrs. Habersham had heard a little about the relationship between Michael and Stephanie Boudreau and could see that Michael was unhappy, but she didn't want to pry. If Michael wanted to talk about Stephanie, she would listen. Although she was curious, her good manners would not allow for anything else.

Later that evening, Michael knocked at the kitchen door of the mansion. He didn't see the senator's sedan or Stephanie's convertible. He hoped Maggie was not busy and had some news for him. She could tell him what was going on in Atlanta, or at least offer him a sandwich. When Maggie let him in, he was surprised to see Stephanie sitting at the table relaxing with a glass of wine in her hand. Without thinking about it, he pulled her out of the chair, put his arms around her, and buried his face in her hair just to breathe in her scent.

Oh, God, his feelings hit him like a ton of bricks. He was deeply in love with this woman. He knew he liked her, was attracted to her, missed her, and there was no doubt that he desperately wanted her, but for the first time he realized that this was the one he wanted to spend the rest of his life with. Boudreau's money wasn't important anymore; nothing mattered except that he had to make her his.

Stephanie was startled. "Whoa, boy," she said as she pulled back, laughing, yet concerned by his almost desperate embrace. She looked at him but was not sure what she read in his face. "Are you okay?"

"Now, I am." Not wanting to let her go, he kissed her. He had missed her so much.

Stephanie pulled back again, trying to catch her breath. "Michael, we are not alone," she whispered, glancing at Maggie who was standing by the sink, wide-eyed, taking it all in.

Michael looked at Maggie and smiled, "Sorry Maggie. It's just that I've missed this girl so much. He looked back at Stephanie, "Sorry, Steph, did I break a rib there?" He turned her loose but kept her hand in his.

"Don't mind me," said Maggie. "I'm just standing here minding my own business. But, Michael, I'm glad you came by. I got something to tell you 'bout the statue."

"What's all this about the statue?" asked Stephanie looking from Maggie to Michael as his face flushed with color.

"Oh, it's nothing. I had asked Maggie some questions about it. Let's go into the parlor and you can tell me about your trip to Atlanta and what the doctor said about the senator's condition." He led Stephanie out of the kitchen, hoping that Maggie would understand that he didn't want to discuss Aphrodite in front of Stephanie.

After sitting next to each other on the comfortable sofa, her hand still in his, Stephanie proceeded to tell Michael what had transpired at the Cancer Clinic at Emory University Hospital. The senator was examined by the head of the department and several tests were done. The diagnosis was the same—lung cancer—but they found the Boudreau in good physical condition otherwise. An operation was recommended, just like the Savannah surgeon had suggested. With chemotherapy and luck, he should recover and be around for a long time. Of course, there were no guarantees, but both Stephanie and her father were encouraged.

Stephanie was still not satisfied and wanted to take him up to a specialist at Duke University Hospital and see if the operation should be done there.

"Daddy doesn't want to go, but I'm going to insist. I won't be happy until we have the very best facility and the best surgeon for him. This is my Daddy we're talking about."

She tried to blink back the tears, but they began to slide

down her cheeks. Michael put her head on his shoulder and let her cry it out. The quiet tears turned to sobs and Michael's shirt became damp. He was wishing he had a handkerchief, when Maggie came in and handed him a box of tissues. Michael's looked up to thank her and saw tears in her eyes, also. He handed several tissues to Stephanie and after a couple of gulps and deep breaths, she stopped crying, closed her eyes and snuggled into his wet shoulder.

Michael picked her up in his arms. "Babe, you're dead tired. You need to sleep. I'm taking you up and put you to bed."

Maggie gave him a sharp look. "Maybe I should come up, too?"

Michael smiled, "No, I promise to behave and won't attack her like I did earlier. I'm just going to take off her shoes and cover her up. She can sleep in the slacks and t-shirt she's wearing."

"Okay, but you watch yo'self, boy. I'll be waiting for you in the kitchen."

Upstairs, Michael turned down the lacy gold and white comforter and lay Stephanie down on the pillows. He slipped off her shoes and covered her with a sheet and a light blanket. He wondered if he should remove her watch and her bracelet but didn't want to awaken her.

He sat on the foot of the bed and just looked at her. She was so beautiful, her raven hair spread across the pillow, her dark lashes curved like miniature fans against her porcelain cheeks. She may look fragile but he knew she had inner strength, which surfaced when she took over her father's health situation. And she was spunky. Michael wished he could forget how she threw him out of her bed the night of the dance. He especially wanted to forget what happed afterwards with Aphrodite.

"Oh, God, what am I going to do?" he asked himself.

Michael carefully pushed Stephanie's hair back from her forehead, brushed his lips against her cheek and went downstairs to talk with Maggie.

When he entered the kitchen, Maggie was preparing a sandwich and a glass of iced tea for him. "I figured you'd be hungry," she said and set it on the table.

"Thank you. This looks good." He sat down at the table and reached for the tea, "I guess you understood that I didn't want to talk about the statue in front of Stephanie. She has too much on her mind right now, and to tell you the truth, I don't know how to explain what happened since I don't understand it myself. I know I have to tell her about Aphrodite sooner or later, but I didn't think she could handle it tonight."

"You're right. My girl's got lots of worry right now. I wasn't thinking. I was excited about what Mama told me. She called this morning to say that her neighbor, George, was having a drink with her the other evening and she told him about the statue."

"He recalled something 'bout a marble statue that was buried in the marsh years ago. He said it sound like Aphrodite when Mama described it. You wanna ride up to Mama's with me tomorrow and talk to George?"

Michael almost choked on his sandwich. He coughed and swallowed and sipped some tea before he could speak. "Is this for real? Who is this George? Can he be believed or is he someone who would make this up? How could a statue like Aphrodite end up on the Carolina marshes?"

"Well now, you're asking lots of questions I can't answer. That's why you need to talk to George. I don't think he would make this up, but there's no telling if his story has anything to do with that evil thing that's in the garden," Maggie shuddered.

"Okay, I want to go with you, but I can't go tomorrow because Phillip's mother is in the hospital and he's taking off a few days. The day after tomorrow is Saturday. Can we go then? If there's even a remote possibility that there is a connection, I want to check it out."

Even though they were very busy in the office without Phillip, the next day dragged for Michael. All he could think of was what Maggie had told him about the statue of Aphrodite. Questions kept going around and around in his head: *Who is this George? Was he making this up to get attention? Could there be a connection between an expensive marble statue and something dug up from the Carolina marshes?*

First thing that morning, he had apologized to Peaches. "I'm sorry about what I said yesterday. As I said before, Phillip is crazy about you, but he's a little naïve and very vulnerable right now. He's such a straight-up guy. I don't want to see him hurt. Can we forget that conversation and be friends?"

Michael put out his hand and after giving him a long look out of those sharp green eyes, Peaches smiled and placed her hand in his. "Okay, I'll let it go for now, but you watch your step, Chicago. I'm not planning to hurt anybody." She walked back to her desk, hips swinging suggestively, and looked at him from over her shoulder. "But, I do looove his house," and she gave him a slow wink.

Michael smiled and shook his head. *Poor Phillip,* he thought. *His life will never be the same, but he will love every minute of it.* He sat at his desk and tried to concentrate on his work.

Chapter 27

"Got some news about that Greek son-of-a-bitch, Andrews," said Steve to Big Duke. "He's turned up in Savannah."

Big Duke looked up from the papers on his desk and lit a cigar, "Where the hell is that? Never heard of it."

"Oh, it's somewhere down south in Georgia.. Here's what I'm thinking. Rocco's going east in a few days to take care of that problem in Miami. Maybe he should stop off in Savannah first and take care of Andrews. The guys at the other casinos are still laughing behind our backs about what happened with the Texans. If we don't discourage stuff like that, more bastards will try to rip us off."

"Yeah, yeah, you're right. Tell Rocco to mess him up good, but not to kill him. We don't want to have a body on our hands in case something goes wrong. Not that there will be any strong police presence in a backward place like Georgia. Still, we don't wanna ask for trouble."

The pit boss was glad to have Big Duke's okay. He had disliked and resented Andrews from day one. He thought

Michael too cocky, too smooth and didn't want to hire him. But hiring Michael had been Big Duke's call and Steve had better sense than to remind his boss of that. He grinned to himself, thinking of Michael with a smashed up face and a few broken bones. He deserved it for making a fool of him.

Steve went downstairs to look for Rocco. He wished he could be there when that smart mouth Greek got what he deserved.

Chapter 28

Boudreau insisted on having his operation in Atlanta at Emory University Hospital. After making arrangements for more tests on Monday, Stephanie decided to drive him up the Saturday before so they could visit with the senator's sister, Catherine, for the weekend.

Maggie was helping them pack the car when Michael came over from the carriage house. He hefted the largest of the suitcases into the trunk of the Cadillac.

"Gee, Steff. How long are you planning to stay—a month?" he joked as he followed her back into the house when she went to get her purse.

"Now, Michael, you know women like to take a lot of clothes when they travel, and since the Caddy has plenty of room, why not? Don't get into any trouble while we are away," she teased.

"Just don't stay too long." He wrapped her into a hug. "Listen, I understand all you can handle right now is your father, but when you get back next week, can we talk? There's so much I want to say to you. God, I'm going to miss you so much."

Stephanie hugged him back but pulled away when he began to tighten his arms around her. She could see he was upset that she was leaving, but she really couldn't think about her feelings for Michael right now.

"Michael, I can't promise you anything. Let's see what the doctor says after reviewing the tests and we'll go from there. Please understand, Daddy has to come first."

When they went back out to the driveway, Boudreau was sitting in the passenger seat, talking to Maggie in a low voice.

"Michael, I've been thinking," said the senator when Michael went to the window to wish him a good trip. "Why don't you move into the house while we're away? There's plenty of room and Maggie tells me she wants to visit her mother while we're gone. I don't like to leave the house unattended."

Michael's eyes went straight to Maggie's. When she nodded, he answered. "Thank you, sir. I'd like that. Being closer to the kitchen and Maggie's good cooking will be great."

After Stephanie and the Senator drove away, Maggie and Michael prepared for their trip to South Carolina.

"I want to go in my car," she said. "Can you bring that basket from the kitchen table out here?"

"Do you want me to drive?" Michael asked, carrying out the large wicker basket Maggie had packed. "I don't mind."

"No, my car's funny. She don't like strangers touching her wheel, 'specially Yankees," she teased. "Besides, I know the way."

They took the bypass to I-16 and drove north over

the Talmadge Bridge across the Savannah River to South Carolina. When they approached the highest point of the bridge, Maggie told Michael to turn his head to the right and look toward Savannah. He was surprised to see how lovely the city looked. It was like looking at a painting hanging on the wall in a museum.

The Savannah River was a wide gray ribbon. A toy ship, herded by a tiny tug, crept toward the ocean. Time-weathered gray buildings facing the river were backed by the bluff and tall live oaks. On the right, the gold dome of City Hall sparkled, and farther back to the left, the steeple of the Cathedral of St. John the Baptist speared the azure blue sky. Other smaller buildings were tucked into the greenery. It could have been a miniature eighteenth century village on a postcard.

"Wow, I didn't know Savannah could look so beautiful. We passed by too fast, though. I'll check it out again on the way back. Thanks for telling me to look."

"Yes, it's a nice view, but you won't be able to see it on the way back. You can only see it going north from the passenger side. Steffie sez she wish she could bring her camera and take pictures, but it's too dangerous to stop the car on the bridge."

Twenty minutes later, Maggie took a narrow two-lane road that cut through an area of dense trees. Every couple of miles, the trees would thin out and Michael could see water and marshes. A few miles after that, there would be hardwood trees and pines again. Eventually, the terrain became totally marshy with shallow water running under a series of small bridges. Finally, they turned into an unpaved road and five or six miles later, they stopped in front of a neat clapboard cabin painted blue with gray shutters. Multi-colored flowers spilled out of pots on the porch and window boxes. About a hundred yards to the left stood a similar cabin. Between the two cabins was a large garden planted with vegetables.

As soon as Maggie stopped the car, Maggie's mother, dressed in a colorful caftan came out on the porch, her hair wrapped in a matching turban. She waited, smiling, as her daughter got out of the car and came up the steps. The two woman embraced as Michael followed with the basket.

"Mama, this is Michael," said Maggie. To Michael, she said, "You can call her Mama Sally."

Keen dark eyes searched Michael's face. He had the feeling that Sally was looking into his very soul. "Welcome," said Mama Sally, offering her hand, which he found soft except for small calluses on the tips of the fingers.

"Thank you for allowing me to come. I see now where Maggie gets her good looks. That's a beautiful dress. The colors are stunning."

"Thank you, Michael. We'll, sit out here on the porch where it's cool." With a graceful hand, she indicated the white rocking chairs. "My girl and me will go inside and get the lunch ready." Making no attempt to lower her voice as she walked inside the cabin, she continued. "Yeah, I see what you mean. He's too smooth and sweet talkin' for Steffie. Fine lookin' man, though, Hmm hmm."

"Mama, shame on you!" Maggie giggled.

After the woman went inside, Michael reached in his pocket and took out a cigarette. He sat in a rocking chair and smoked for a few minutes, enjoying the peaceful, verdant vista. Golden sunlight filtered through the leaves that swished softly in the breeze. He heard the buzzing of insects, the melodious trill of birds and smelled the sweet scent of flowers. *What a wonderful little slice of paradise,* he thought.

Suddenly, he jumped up from the chair. *Good God, all this quiet would drive him crazy in less than 24 hours.* He stepped down from the porch and went to explore.

When he approached the garden between the two cabins, he was amazed at what he saw. There were rows and rows of green beans, squash, cucumbers, salad greens, carrots, and both red and green peppers. Toward the back, there were tomatoes tied to stakes and even tall stalks of corn. The rows were neat and weed free. Someone had done a lot of work. He didn't think Mama Sally could handle this garden by herself.

Looking toward the second cabin, Michael noticed two brown and white spotted hound dogs sleeping on the porch. He was surprised that the dogs hadn't even barked when they drove up. But now, responding to some unheard signal, the dogs got up and stood facing the door of the cabin.

The screen door opened and a wizened old black man wearing bib overalls came out. He was whip-thin, and no more than five feet five inches tall. He picked up an old straw hat from one of the chairs on the porch, slapped it on his head and came down toward Michael. As the old man got closer, Michael could see his face was latticed with wrinkles but his eyes were sharp and clear.

"Hello," Michael greeted him. "I'm a friend of Maggie's from Savannah. My name is Michael Andrews and I have to say, this is the most amazing garden I've ever seen. Who does all this work?"

Hitching his thumbs in his overall straps, he looked

up at Michael, "I do. Well, Sally, she he'p some, but I does it mostly. Yep, it's looking purty good this year," he said proudly. "Weather's been good. Jus' 'nough rain. I'm George." He stuck out a skinny arm with ropy muscles ending in a calloused hand. Michael was surprised at the strength of his grip.

"But, what do you do with all this produce? You and Sally can't possibly eat it all, and I don't see any other houses around."

"Oh, I takes it to Chas'ton market in my truck twice a week and sells it. It he'ps pay the bills." At a loss in what to say next, Michael was saved by Maggie's appearance on Sally's porch, waving them inside for lunch.

After a delicious lunch of baked ham, biscuits, red rice, and some of just about every vegetable growing in the garden, they sat out on Sally's porch and sipped more sweet tea, served with peach cobbler. Michael thought he would explode, but turned down nothing he was offered. When the women took the last plate and glass inside to be washed, Michael asked George what he knew about the marble statue.

George reached into the pocket of his overalls and pulled out a pipe and a pouch of tobacco. "Way-all," he drawled as he filled his pipe. "When I wuz small, there wuz a dozen cabins here, and in the evenin's we all set together and tell stories. The story 'bout the statue was just a made up story far as I knew 'til Maggie tole me 'bout the statue in Savannah. If there's any truth to the story I's gonna tell, you hafta decide that fo' yo'sef."

George sat back in his chair and puffed on his pipe. "The way it was tole to me, is that a long, long time ago, a group of folks were brought to a place in Florida from across the ocean by some rich men from England. The folks come from different countries. They wuz white, but treated like slaves, anyhow, and made to work in the fields to grow rice and t'baccy. They work very hard but didn't get much food so most got sick and died. The ones that lived ran away and moved to a place close to St. Augustine.

"There wuz lots of pirates and smugglin' going on back then and some ships sunk close to the shore and lots of stuff washed up on the beach. Somebody found a statue half covered with sand and 'cause the crew died on the ship and some other bad things happen, folks began to think that the statue was witched. The leaders took the statue to the woods and left it there, but the folks who like the statue found out where it wuz and they go back and talk to it and ask for favors 'cause they b'lieved the statue had powers.

"Some years later, a priest of Jesus, he come there for the people. When he found out about the statue, he say it was evil and tole them to get shed of it or they wouldn't go to heaven. The people took it and buried it in the marsh but would fetch it up once a year and have a kind of party. They drink and smoke some kind of weed and dance 'round the statue. Some said the statue spoke to 'em. One day, there come a turrible hurricane and when they look for the statue after the storm, it gone."

"Long time after, some folks 'round here, Gullah they wuz, found a beautiful marble lady in the marsh. Maybe the storm blew it here. But something bad seem to happen to anyone who touch it, so when a man from Savannah come 'round who buy old stuff, they give him the statue. They didn't want no money. They 'fraid and was glad to be shed of it."

Michael's eyes never once left the old man's face. When George finished, he realized his mouth was dry and his heart was racing. This story had to have some truth to it. Michael remembered what Mrs. Habersham said about the Greek Shrine in St. Augustine. Could there be a connection? He noticed Maggie had come out on the porch and heard part of the story. Her eyes were wide with fear.

"Thank you for the story, George. It could very well explain the statue of Aphrodite that's in Senator Boudreau's garden. When he gets back from Atlanta, I'll ask him where he bought it. I haven't wanted to bother him, but now that we have a Florida–Georgia connection, I have some clues to follow."

Michael looked up at the sky that had turned from bright blue to dull gray. "Maggie, if you're ready, I think we better head for Savannah. Dark clouds are gathering and we don't want to be caught in a flash flood on one of those little bridges."

Maggie blinked and pulled out of the trance she was in, "Yes, yes, you're right. We better start for home."

Goodbyes were said. Michael shook George's hand and thanked him again for the story. As Maggie and Michael walked to the car, Maggie whispered, "Michael, do you mind driving back? I feel a little shaky."

Chapter 29

On Monday afternoon, Michael left work as quickly as he could, anxious to go to the Historical Society Library to tell Mrs. Habersham what he had learned in South Carolina. He parked on a side street a block away and ran up the steps of the library two at a time. Mrs. Habersham looked up from behind the desk and smiled as he burst through the door. One look at his flushed and excited face told her he had some information to share about the statue.

"Hello, Michael. You must have had some good news this weekend."

"Yes, I did, but let me catch my breath," he panted. "I ran most of the way here and up all eighteen of the steps to the door. Whew, I must be out of shape."

"Here, sit down at the table. I have some information for you, also. But, I suspect yours is more exciting than mine."

After taking a few deep breaths, Michael related what he had learned on the trip to the South Carolina low country, specifically the story told by the old man, George. He left out the part about the statue having supernatural powers, but otherwise repeated it pretty much as George told it. When he finished, he looked at Mrs. Habersham and waited for her reaction.

Mrs. Habersham was as excited as Michael. "This is absolutely amazing, Michael. Remember the information that I requested from St. Augustine? They referred me to research done by Dr. E.P. Panagopoulos, who is compiling information for a book about a colony established in 1768 south of St. Augustine."

"Does it seem to correlate with what I heard from George?" asked Michael.

"Yes, the information I received states that a group of settlers from Europe, many of them Greeks, were brought to an area in Florida, seventy-five miles south of St. Augustine. It was a commercial venture, headed by Dr. Andrew Turnbull and sponsored by Great Britain, to produce crops, such as olives, cotton, and tobacco to be sent back to England for sale. The story closely parallels the one George told you, except there is no mention of a statue in the old documents."

"The colonists, about 1,400 in number, were brought to an area called New Smyrna, named for Turnbull's Greek wife, who was from Smyrna in Asia Minor. In fact, nine hundred and sixty-four workers died of disease and starvation. After nine years, the remaining colonists escaped to St. Augustine and were given their freedom by the Spanish governor."

Michael was stunned. The information was too similar not to be connected. He would talk to the senator first chance he had to ask him where, and from whom, he had purchased the statue of Aphrodite.

"I think it's the same statue, Mrs. Habersham. What do you think?"

"It could very well be. Let's see what Senator Boudreau has to say. You'll let me know, won't you?" Mrs. Habersham was happy that the mystery may be solved, but the librarian had become fond of Michael and was sorry that his visits would end.

"Mrs. Habersham, Do you think it possible that a pirate ship capsized near the shore of the New Smyrna colony and the statue sank in the water to eventually end up on the beach? Then, sometime later, could a hurricane blow it north to the South Carolina marshlands?"

"Well, yes, it's possible, but I don't think we'll ever know for sure."

Michael thanked Mrs. Habersham and gave her a quick hug. He promised to call as soon as he talked with the senator. Driving home, he mulled over what he had learned about Aphrodite's possible connection to St. Augustine. Maybe he wasn't crazy after all. There was no doubt in his mind that the statue had unnatural powers. But how dangerous was it and how was he to get rid of it before it ruined his life?

Chapter 30

The senator's Cadillac was in the drive when Michael came home from work several days later, which meant the senator and Stephanie were back from Atlanta. He went up to his apartment and called Stephanie to tell her how much he had missed her and to ask if the senator felt like having company.

"I think he would like to have you visit. He's missed your man-to-man discussions. But, you can't smoke around him. The doctor said fifty years of smoking cigarettes and cigars is what probably gave him the cancer. Come into the study in about forty-five minutes. He should be up from his nap by then."

Avoiding the garden, Michael went out to the front portico to wait. He reached into his pocket for his pack of cigarettes and then changed his mind. Suddenly, he didn't have the taste for a smoke. Maybe he should cut down. He sat on the wrought iron bench, his head bent, his hands hanging between his knees, thinking of how to approach the senator about the statue of Aphrodite.

After a few minutes, Stephanie came out to the portico. She looked pale and thin. Michael's heart ached when he saw the dark smudges under her beautiful hazel eyes. He stood up and took her in his arms and gently rubbed her back. She rested her head against his chest and circled his waist with her arms, breathing in his strength.

"You can go to see him," she said, pulling away to look at his face. "But, I want to talk to you first. Here's where we stand. I took him to Emory and called Duke University Hospital. After lengthy conversations with doctors at both hospitals, it was agreed that he could have the operation in Atlanta at Emory, which is what Daddy wanted all along. The doctors assured me that follow-up treatments, like radiation and chemo, can be done here in Savannah just as well. This way, he won't get worn out with the travel. He's in good health, otherwise, and they think he has a good chance for remission, but there is no guarentee."

"Michael, I am terribly frightened. I can't imagine being without Daddy. He's the only parent I've ever had. I know I will lose him someday, but please, God, not just yet." Tears, like miniature pearls, ran down her cheeks.

Michael pulled her back into his embrace and kissed her hair. "I'm here for you, baby, just tell me what I can do to help."

"Right now, you can go into the study and cheer him up. He's seen no one but Maggie and me and the doctors for the last few days. Talk to him about what's going on downtown or maybe about his boat." She blinked her eyes, trying to control her tears. "I'll be in the kitchen with Maggie."

Pasting a smile on his face, he walked into the study to find Boudreau sitting behind his desk, his chair swiveled around looking out at his garden. When he turned, the senator's face was pale and drawn. Michael tried not to show his concern.

"How's it going, Senator? I've missed our dinners together and our discussions about sports and politics. I guess it's been about a week since I've seen you."

"I've missed you, too. I've been poked, prodded and turned inside out by a whole bevy of doctors and nurses. I think they've finally come to a decision about what to do for me. Don't know if Steffie told you, but I'm going to Atlanta for the operation and then get treatments here in Savannah. That suits me since I don't want to be away from home any longer than I have to."

"Sit down, boy. I know Stephanie sent you in to cheer me up, but we need to do some serious talking." Boudreau looked at Michael, studying his face before he continued. "I want you to understand our oral contract is still in force. I've spoken to my lawyer and it's now part of my will that you will get what I promised when you marry Stephanie. Now that I've gotten to know you, I feel sure you will take care of her."

The senator grabbed the edge of the desk and stood up, his face red and his eyes burning with passion. "But, let me assure you, if you hurt my daughter in any way, I'll find some way back from the grave, and you won't like what I do to you."

Michael rose from the chair and faced the senator, his voice filled with emotion. "No, Senator, you can forget what we talked about weeks ago. Things have changed."

Boudreau's complexion went from angry red to pasty white in seconds. "What do you mean? You promised to take

care of Stephanie. She needs someone to take care of her."
He sat down heavily in his chair.

"You're mistaken, Senator. Stephanie is a strong young woman, as strong as the live oak trees growing all around Savannah. Look how she has taken care of you. Believe me, she can take care of herself. But, let me explain. You don't have to worry about Stephanie because I love her and I want her— not your money. If she will have me, I want to be with her the rest of my life. I don't want to push her right now because she's concerned about you. All you need to do is take care of yourself and get well, because if I have my way, in a few years you'll have grandchildren to take out in that fancy boat of yours."

For a few seconds, Boudreau's face was inscrutable, then, he broke out in a big grin. "You Greek son-of-a-gun. You scared me to death—even before the doctors could do me in. Come over here and shake my hand!"

His grin as large as the senator's, Michael went to the older man and grabbed him in a hug. "Screw the handshake," he said, "We Greeks aren't ashamed to show our emotions. But, I won't kiss you. That would shake you up too much."

This was how Stephanie found them, with their arms around each other and smiles on their faces. She didn't even ask what had happened. She was just content to see her father looking happy for the first time in weeks.

"Daddy, Maggie has some delicious chicken soup for you in the kitchen." Looking a little embarrassed, Boudreau pulled away from Michael and hurried out of the room.

Stephanie turned to Michael. "I don't know what you said to him, but thank you for cheering him up. He's been very depressed and it was wonderful to see him smile." She laughed, "I've never seen him hug a man before. What was all that about?"

"Nothing you need to know about right now, but you'll find out one of these days." He crossed the room, put his arms around her, and rubbed his face in her hair. She smelled so fresh, so sweet. God, how he wanted her. It was driving him crazy. He pulled back and looked at her closely.

"Look, what is the time schedule for the operation? When will you be going back to Atlanta?"

"We have a few days yet. Daddy still has some tests to finish here. The results will go with us when we go to Emory. His hospital stay will be from three to five days, depending how he responds to the surgery. Why do you ask?"

"I have to go to St. Augustine. To…uh, meet some people who are planning a big banquet at the hotel. Would it be possible for you go with me? Won't the senator be all right with Maggie for a couple of days?" He rubbed her shoulders.

"Baby, you are wound up tight as a spring. You need to relax and I would love to have you go with me. I understand St. Augustine is a lovely little town and we can do some sightseeing—among other things."

Stephanie didn't pretend to misunderstand his meaning. His incredible eyes were burning with desire and she could feel the answering response in her tightening breasts and belly.

"I don't know," she whispered, "but I'll see if I can work it out. I'll talk to Maggie." She slipped out of his arms. "There's plenty of hot chicken soup in the kitchen if you're hungry."

He followed her to the kitchen, muttering, "I'm hungry all right, but hot soup isn't what will satisfy me right now."

Chapter 31

S enator Boudreau and Maggie agreed it was a good idea for Stephanie to go to Florida with Michael. He asked for a couple of days off from work, so on a bright sunshiny morning, they put down the top of the convertible and started south on I-95 for the four-hour ride to St. Augustine. Stephanie pushed the worry about her father to the back of her mind, leaned her head back on the seat and closed her eyes. When traffic thinned out on the highway, Michael drove with his left hand on the wheel, using his right to hold Stephanie's hand.

While Stephanie rested, Michael was running scenarios through his mind. *How to tell Stephanie about Aphrodite? What had happened was so bizarre, so unbelievable, what would she think? How could he make her believe it? Should he tell her what he found out from George?*

When they arrived at the motel where Michael had made reservations, he parked the car and reached for Stephanie before she could climb out. "Steffie, I only reserved one room, but it you are not comfortable with that, I'll ask for another."

BESS T. CHAPPAS

She turned and smiled at his hopeful face. "No, one room, one bed is all we need." The trust in her beautiful hazel eyes calmed his anxious heart and it overflowed with love. The thought of them in bed together was something he dreamed about every night, but he didn't want to rush her.

After they brought their bags into the room Michael suggested they go out to get some lunch. They asked the receptionist at the desk for the name of a good restaurant and she directed them to an Italian bistro. The food was good but neither one had an appetite. The looks between them were so hot they could have lit up the entire town of St. Augustine. After a few attempts to eat, Stephanie placed her fork on her plate and looked at Michael.

"Let's go back to the motel," she whispered.

When they arrived at their room, Michael shut the door and leaned against it. His knees were weak and his hands were shaking. He almost smiled to himself. The great lover, who could get any woman he wanted, was as nervous as a teenager anticipating his first sexual experience. He wanted Stephanie so badly, he was afraid he would not be able to control himself.

Stephanie walked to the middle of the room and turned to face him, her eyes, shining golden orbs, her mouth rosy and wet. She began to unbutton her shirt and let it slide to the floor. Stepping out of her jeans, she kicked off her sandals, and stood looking at him wearing only a lacy bra and bikini underpants. Nervously, her tongue darted out and licked her top lip.

Michael was so hard, he was in pain. He closed the space between them and scooped her up and laid her across

— 146 —

the bed. He quickly undressed down to his shorts and sat down beside her. He started kissing her hair, her cheeks, her mouth, her neck, down to the swell of her breast above the restraining bra. Her skin was like silk, so soft, so smooth, so fragrant.

"Stephanie, you are so beautiful. I've wanted you from the very first time I saw you. Please let me see all of you."

Stephanie smiled and pushed him aside as she reached behind and unhooked her bra and tossed it to the floor along with her panties. She sighed as Michael's large hands gently closed around her breasts and his thumb flicked across the rosy tips causing them to tighten and pucker. When he put his mouth on the distended tip and suckled, Stephanie felt the responding ache in her belly.

His kisses continued to travel downward to her stomach, then lower to just above the silky bush of dark curls at the juncture of her thighs. Stephanie ran her hands over Michael's strong muscular shoulders. She explored his chest, feeling the crinkly hair that arrowed down to his shorts. She pulled him down on top and raised her hips, bringing his hardness fully against her moist center. She started to slip her hand under the elastic of his shorts when he grabbed her hand.

"God, Steffie, I want you to touch me, but if you do right now, it will all be over."

Feeling his control start to dissolve, he spread her legs and put his mouth on her, bringing her to a startling orgasm. Then he pulled off his shorts, entered her in one quick thrust and allowed himself to join her in a mind-crunching orgasm.

Later, Stephanie awoke slowly. She felt wonderful but

wasn't sure why. Then she remembered. She smiled and raised her arms and stretched like a contended feline. She looked at the other side of the bed expecting to see Michael, but he wasn't there. Had it been a dream? But no, there was an indentation on the pillow next to her and she could see his suitcase across the room.

Before she could wonder where he was, she heard the lock on the door and Michael came in with a small tray of coffee, juice and Danish. Setting the tray on the bedside table, he took Stephanie in his arms and kissed her deeply.

"Good morning, Gorgeous. I brought food to give you some strength. We're not anywhere near finished."

Stephanie reached for the coffee. "We're not? I thought last night was wonderful. I'm sorry that I'm not very experienced, but I thought…."

"Baby, you were just perfect. It's just that I had waited so long, it was way too fast. Finish your coffee and I will show you how it should be done -slow and easy." And he did.

Much later, they slept again.

A loud noise woke Stephanie. It sounded like a fire truck or an ambulance outside the motel room. Michael was snoring softly in her ear, his arms around her waist and his legs wrapped around hers. She slowly entangled herself and slipped off the bed, collecting her clothes that were strewn around the room. Peeking through the curtain, she was surprised that it was dark outside. Her watch on the dresser said it was 8:30 p.m. Heavens, they had been in bed all day. She looked at herself in the bathroom mirror. Her hair was a mess, her makeup smeared, and she needed a bath. She was a bit sore, but her eyes were shinning and there was a smile on her face.

Remembering what had happened in bed with Michael, a giggle escaped her and she quickly put her hand over her mouth. *What's wrong with me,* she wondered. *I never giggle.*

After a long hot shower and wearing only a towel, she came out of the bathroom to search for fresh clothes from her suitcase. Michael was sitting up in bed drinking the tepid orange juice he had brought in hours ago. His eyes devoured her.

"There she is, all damp and sexy, smelling of perfumed soap. Why don't you come closer and let me give you a good morning kiss."

"Oh, no, I'm staying away from you until you take a shower. Although I have to say I like that disheveled look, with your hair in your eyes and a bit of beard on your handsome face. I have to admit you look better than I did when I woke up. Hurry up. Let's go out and get something to eat. I'm starving."

After a delicious seafood dinner, they walked arm in arm, enjoying each other and the warmth of the summer night. They strolled in and out of the shops, but purchased nothing. They walked to the bay where the half moon reflected in the water like a shinning mirror and stars circled the moon like a million sparkling diamonds.

Michael and Stephanie were so engrossed in each other they didn't notice the store clerks and tourists smiling at the lovely willowy dark-haired girl and the tall handsome man at her side. *Ah, young love,* they sighed.

The next morning, under pretense of having to meet the group that wanted to meet at the DeSoto Hotel in Savannah, Michael went to the St. Augustine Historical Society while Stephanie packed. The visit was disappointing because they had little additional information about the Turnbull project. The director at the Historical Society promised to forward any new information he could find to Mrs. Habersham in Savannah.

When they stopped in Jacksonville for lunch, Stephanie was ravenous. She ordered a big lunch and cleaned her plate.

"Wow, I've never seen you eat so much," said Michael. "Keep it up so you can put back on some of the weight you lost worrying about the senator. I wouldn't mind if you gain a few pounds. Just more for me to love."

"Well, I did get a lot of exercise in St. Augustine," she said, blushing a little. Michael just smiled, thinking about their lovemaking.

Back in the car, as they drove closer to Savannah, Stephanie's mood became troubled. The time with Michael had been wonderful, but she became overcome with anxiety when she thought about her father's illness. She was worried about the senator's operation and the difficult treatments afterwards. She felt guilty for leaving him, even though she knew he was in good hands with Maggie. She drew away from Michael and leaned closer to the car window.

What was I thinking, getting so tangled up with this guy? Stephanie wondered. *I shouldn't have left my father, but Michael is so hard to resist. He is so handsome and sexy, with those fantastic eyes that can cast a spell. I didn't know sex could be like that. It wasn't anything like I experienced with Spencer.*

That night at the dance, I wondered how we would fit physically and now I know we fit perfectly. But, it's not just the spectacular sex. He's fun to be with, yet, he is so sweet and loving he makes me feel like a goddess. He made sure that my pleasure came first and treats me so special. It's strange, but I feel comfortable with him, as if I have known him forever. Somehow, I trust him, even though he could leave tomorrow and head back to Chicago or even fly to Europe.

I'm pretty sure I heard him say, "I love you" when we were making love, but a man will say anything in the throes of passion. Maybe, I just wanted to hear it because I think I may be in love with him. Being with Michael is fantastic, yet I'm confused and a little frightened because I'm not sure I can survive another broken heart. I need to be strong to take care of Daddy.

Michael sensed Stephanie was troubled, but wasn't sure what to say to her. He hoped she wasn't sorry they had made love. Being with her had meant the world to him because he was desperately in love with her. He had to tell her how he felt and needed her to understand how important these two days had been for him. He realized he had nothing to offer her, but he would change and become the man she deserved. He wasn't sure how at this point, but living the rest of his life without Stephanie was unthinkable. That was one of the reasons he wanted her with him in St. Augustine, away from the senator and Maggie but he wasn't sure she understood how deep his feelings were.

The other reason was to tell her about the statue of Aphrodite, but how to explain that? He didn't even understand it himself. She would think he had lost his mind. The only one who believed him was Maggie. How odd that she would be his only ally, when just a few weeks ago, she hated and mistrusted him.

His research on the early Greek settlers at the St. Augustine Historical Society had been a disappointment. They had little information on the New Smyrna colony. The site of the old Spanish Mission in St. Augustine that had taken in the runaways was recently purchased by the Greek Orthodox Church to be used as a shrine to honor the first Greeks who landed in America. Nothing had been discovered that answered any of his questions about the statue. He couldn't bring himself to tell her about Aphrodite and spoil their wonderful time together.

They continued north on I-95 in the warm summer evening. On their left, pumpkin-colored clouds streaked the sky, heralding the descent of the hazy sun. As the sky darkened, tall southern pines and live oaks cocooned them on the highway, with only an occasional car rushing past like a giant insect, headlights blazing. Michael noticed Stephanie rubbing her arms so he pushed the knob that brought down the top of the convertible. By the time they reached the senator's mansion, darkness had fallen. Michael drove into the circular driveway and turned off the motor.

Busy with their thoughts, neither moved for several seconds. The scent of magnolia and jasmine mixed cloyingly with the humid air and the chirp of the tree frogs and rustle of other night creatures seemed surprisingly loud in the dark.

When Stephanie made a move to open the car door, Michael placed his hand on her arm. "Please, Steffie, before we go in, can I talk to you for a few minutes?" Stephanie slipped one long, slim leg underneath her and turned toward him.

"These two days have been the most wonderful days of my life. Being with you, holding you, loving you has been a dream come true. Steffie, I want you to know that I am in love with you, truly and deeply in love. I've never told another woman I loved her, because I never have been in love before. I didn't even know what love was until I met you. Now, I understand that love is wanting be with someone always, to have a life with that someone, which means marriage and a family."

He shook his head and smiled. "My father would have a heart attack if he heard me say this, but I want a life like my parents have. They've been married for over thirty years and they're still in love."

"Oh, Michael, please don't…"

Michael gently put his hands on her shoulders. "No, just listen. You don't have to say anything now, but I need to say this. I've made many mistakes. I hurt my parents, resented my brother, bummed around the country, drank too much, messed around with drugs, but I will change. I have already changed. Don't you see? You have changed me. I want to be worthy of you and when I think I have something to offer, I will ask you to be my wife."

Stephanie was unsure what to reply to such a serious declaration, but then his eyes change from earnest to playful. "I don't want to frighten you. I just want to stake my claim and let you know that I will continue telling you how much I love you until I wear you down."

Stephanie smiled back at him, "Oh, Michael, you must

know I care for you or I wouldn't have spent these two days with you, so intimately. I love being with you, but this is not the time to make promises. There's Daddy to be taken care of and we really have not known each other very long. Can we just say we're going together and see what happens?"

Michael was disappointed but realized it was not the time to say anything else. Leaving the luggage in the car until morning, they walked up to the front door, put their arms around each other and kissed deeply. Stephanie pushed away from him so she could take a breath.

"Um, Michael, there's a light in the kitchen. Daddy and Maggie must be there waiting for us."

"Sure," he said, understanding she was embarrassed by the thought of facing her father and Maggie.

When they walked into the kitchen, two pair of eyes snapped quickly toward them. Stephanie's face turned crimson and Michael couldn't look at the senator in the eye. Boudreau tried to hide a smile and held out his arms to his daughter. Maggie's heart gave a little twitch sensing the aura of love around the pair, praying that Steffie would not be hurt again.

Then, there was much hugging and shaking of hands and the young couple began to tell about their trip.

Well, so much for playing it cool, thought Michael.

Chapter 32

After sharing one of Maggie's delicious dinners, the Senator went up to bed and Maggie retired to her own cozy den in another part of the house, leaving Michael and Stephanie alone to say good-night. Michael put his arms around Stephanie and pressed his face into her neck to breathe her in.

"Steffie, I can't bear to leave you here and go to my cold bed all alone. Can't you come up and stay a while? We don't know how long you will be in Atlanta and I will be here in Savannah all by myself."

Stephanie took his face between her hands and kissed his eyes and then his mouth. "I think you'll manage very well," she smiled, "but I don't want to leave you either. I'll go upstairs, take a shower, change into something comfortable, and come over." Michael gave her a long kiss and went out the door.

Thirty minutes later, Stephanie tip-toed into her father's room. He was sleeping on his side as was his habit, snoring softly. In repose his face looked young and carefree without the lines between his eyebrows and dark circles beneath his eyes that had gathered there since his illness. She wanted to kiss his forehead, but was afraid he would awaken.

Outside the house, the stars in the sky were competing with the half-moon. The night air was warm and fragrant as she crossed the garden, wearing shorts and a light summer blouse. Her sandals made a soft chuffing sound on the walkway. As she started past the statue of Aphrodite, she paused. It was such a warm evening, yet she shivered as she crossed the garden.

Continuing to Michael's door, she experienced a strange sensation, as if some force was pushing or pulling her toward the statue. As Stephanie stumbled toward the statue, she thought Aphrodite appeared odd, changed somehow. The statue's head had turned and its eyes, red and glowing, were looking at her. Stephanie was confused. Was she losing her mind? Her body felt heavy; her legs couldn't seem hold her up. An ominous darkness surrounded her and only the statue stood out in a weird light. She moved slowly closer and closer to Aphrodite until the darkness enveloped her and she was spinning down, down…

Michael had been watching for Stephanie out of the window of the carriage house. When he saw her come out the side door and walk toward the garden, he went down the stairs to let her in. He opened the door to a sight his mind, at first, could not comprehend. He saw Stephanie slowly stumbling toward Aphrodite. The statue's face was twisted in fury and the eyes were blood red. He had never felt such terror. For a couple of seconds, he couldn't breathe, he couldn't move.

When Stephanie sank to the ground, he ran out, picked her up in his arms and held her close. Michael glared at the statue, his face flushed with anger.

"Don't you dare hurt this girl, you damn bitch. I swear I will take a sledge hammer and beat you to bits. And that's a promise."

Giving a silent prayer of thanks that he could feel Stephanie's heart beating against his chest, he carried her upstairs and laid her on the bed. Her face was bone white and cold to the touch. When she began to tremble, Michael grabbed the blanket from the foot of the bed and wrapped it around her. Then he took off his jeans and shirt and climbed into bed and held her close, trying to warm her with the heat from his body. Attempting to waken her, he rubbed her arms and her back. He gently kissed her cheeks, her eyes and her cold lips.

"Steffie, honey, please wake up. I won't let that bitch hurt you. Please baby, open your eyes."

After a few minutes—although it felt like hours to Michael—Stephanie moaned and opened her eyes. At first, she looked confused and then there was recognition.

"What happened, Michael? Where am I? Why am I so cold?" She wrapped her arms around him and snuggled her head into the curve of his shoulder.

"You're here with me, Steffie, and you're okay. You're safe. I promise I won't let anything happen to you." He held her until she fell asleep again. But there was no rest for Michael that night. He was too frightened to close his eyes. What was he to do? How could he keep Stephanie safe? Thank heaven she was leaving for Atlanta in the morning.

At first light, Michael quietly left the bed, dressed and went downstairs to the garden. The statue of Aphrodite looked normal. This morning, it was just a piece of marble carved into a beautiful woman. Had both he and Stephanie experienced some kind of weird psychotic encounter? No, something had happened last night and Aphrodite had caused it. He was convinced the statue was possessed and dangerous. He had to warn Stephanie. After what happened last night, maybe she will believe him now.

When Michael climbed back up the stairs to the apartment, he put on a pot of coffee. Then, he sat on the side of the bed where Stephanie was still sleeping. She lay on her stomach, her lush fall of dark hair spread out like a fan on the pillow. He leaned down and ran his fingers through its silky length and softly kissed her forehead. She mumbled something and turned on her back, tossing one slim arm over her eyes. When he kissed the creamy underside of her arm, she smiled and stretched. Her eyes opened suddenly and looked straight into his.

"Michael, Oh, my God! What the hell happened last night?"

"Let me bring us both some coffee and I'll tell you what I know about the statue."

While Michael went to get the coffee, Stephanie went to the bathroom to take a quick shower. She didn't have any fresh clothes to put on, so Michael gave her one of his shirts. Then, they both sat on the bed and Michael told her how he had first noticed that the statue had turned around, but that the senator laughed at him. He explained about the trip to Mama Sally's island with Maggie and the story George shared with them. He told her about the research at the library and about the New Smyrna project.

He didn't tell Stephanie about the erotic dream—God,

he hoped it had been a dream—that he experienced with Aphrodite the night of the dance. He just couldn't bring himself to tell her.

Stephanie listened with increasing fear, forgetting her coffee after the first sip. "Oh, Michael, if I had not had that frightening experience last night, I would think you were crazy. But something very strange happened last night and I can't discount it. It was as if the statue took me over, controlled me. I wish now that I had been wearing the *wanga* bag Maggie gave me. Maggie has always said the statue is evil, but we didn't believe her. Can't we just have someone carry it away, throw it in the Savannah River or something?"

"I thought of that, but now that the statue tried to hurt you, I am afraid to touch it, or have anyone else touch it. Meanwhile, you can wear the amulet my Yiayia gave me. I never believed it had any power, even though I promised her I would keep it."

"No, you keep your grandmother's amulet. It was made especially for you. I have the *wanga* bag in my room. I'll wear it until we leave for Atlanta."

"I know this sounds weird, but maybe because the statue is possessed with old evil, these old protectors, like my grandmother's amulet and Maggie's grandmother's *wanga* can help. I feel foolish wearing the amulets, but what can it hurt? I'll be unhappy without you but I think it best that you go to Atlanta today. While you are gone, I'll find a way to get rid of Aphrodite. I'm going back to South Carolina to talk to old George and Maggie's mother again. Maybe they have some suggestions."

After the senator woke up and had a late breakfast, Michael helped Stephanie pack Boudreau's car. When he had a moment alone with the senator, he asked, "I'm just curious, Senator, where did you get that statue in the garden? Did you buy it locally?"

"I purchased it when we bought this house as a tribute to my late wife, Amanda, because she loved the Greek myths. And, yes, I bought it here locally in Savannah, at an antique shop run by a man who is no longer in business. Actually, the man's name was Williams, and he went to prison, accused of murdering another man. It's an interesting story. I'll tell you about it sometime. But, why do you ask about the statue?"

"No particular reason, just wondering."

A few minutes later, Stephanie and her father were on their way to Atlanta to stay with Boudreau's sister, Catherine, until the operation. After his surgery, they planned to stay in Atlanta until the senator was strong enough for the trip back home. Again, the senator asked Michael to stay in the mansion while he and Stephanie were away.

"I would feel more comfortable if Maggie were not alone," he said.

Chapter 33

Michael and Maggie went into the kitchen, each occupied with their own thoughts. Maggie busied herself with making lunch and Michael thought of how to tell the housekeeper what had transpired last night in the garden. Maggie poured him a fresh cup of coffee and set a ham and cheese sandwich with potato salad in front of Michael.

"This gonna be enough for you? I have cake, too." Michael nodded. "I sure am worried about the senator. I don't know how my girl will survive if somethin' happen to him." She poured herself coffee and sat down across the table from Michael.

"I think the senator will be okay. He's pretty tough. As for Steffie, she'll be fine, because no matter what happens, I'll take care of her. You're no fool, Maggie. You know I'm serious about her."

"Hmm. You say you serious. You serious 'bout her or 'bout the senator's money?"

Michael put down his sandwich and looked at Maggie, his eyes burning with anger. "Don't you even think something like that, much less say it out loud. It's her I want. The senator's money can go to hell!"

Don't get excited," she smirked. "Just testin' you."

"Maggie, stop your kidding and listen. Something very scary happened last night in the garden and I need to tell you about it."

Maggie immediately stopped smiling and put her cup down with a shaky hand. "Oh, no! I knew it! I knew something bad was gonna happen. What did that devil statue do?"

"Calm down, Maggie, and listen. After you and the senator went to bed, Steffie planned to come over to the carriage house to…uh…spend some time with me. I was waiting for her downstairs at the door when I saw her stop and look at the statue. She told me later that Aphrodite seemed to be pulling at her and that the statue's face was twisted and its eyes were red. What I saw was Stephanie walking slowly toward Aphrodite and then, she crumbled to the ground in a faint. I have never been so frightened in my life. I ran out and picked her up and took her upstairs. It seemed forever until she came to. She didn't remember what happened until this morning."

Michael left the table and paced around the room, unable to keep still, thinking of what had happened the night before. "I have to get rid of that damn statue, but I'm not sure how."

Maggie's eyes grew big with fright. "Oh, Lordy, I knew that evil statue was gonna hurt my baby. I gave my *wanga* bag to Steffie, but I think she was goin' to get the senator to wear it. I gotta go home tomorrow and see if Granny left any more of her stuff with Mama."

"Stephanie said she would wear the amulet you gave her, but you may want another for yourself." Michael didn't mention his Yiayia's charm he had slipped around his neck this morning. "Can you wait until the weekend so I can go with you? I want to talk to George again in case he's remembered something else. I've been gone two days from work. Can't ask for more time off. Surely you can wait until Sunday."

"I guess so if we have to. I'm not gonna get anywhere near that garden until you figure out a way to get rid of that cursed statue."

Early Sunday morning, Maggie had a basket of food ready when Michael came into the kitchen. Pouring him a cup of coffee, she said, "Don't look like you got much sleep last night. What you want for breakfast?"

"No, didn't sleep well at all. I kept dreaming about what happened the other night with Stephanie and that monster statue. I'd like to beat it into dust and throw the dust in the river, but don't know what will happen if I try something like that. As far as food, Maggie, anything you make will be all right. In fact, I'm not really hungry. I'll just have some cold cereal to make it easy for you."

"Cold cereal? Not in my kitchen. Won't take two minutes to do up some eggs and I done made biscuits to take some with us. A big boy like you needs hot food for breakfast and I love to cook for folks who like to eat."

"Why, Maggie," Michael couldn't help but tease, "A few weeks ago, you wanted to put one of your granny's curses on me and now you're worried I'm not getting enough to eat. Why is that?"

"Don't you get smart with me, boy. You know why. Long as you keep my baby happy, I'll be glad to cook for you, but if you give her any misery, you better check your food 'fore you eat it." She slipped the plate of eggs and biscuits in front of Michael with a wicked grin.

The sun was high in the indigo sky when they reached Mama Sally's island. They found Maggie's mother and George relaxing on the porch of Sally's cabin enjoying a cool drink.

"Come on up and I'll fix you some sweet tea," called Mama Sally.

Michael carried the basket up the steps, shook hands with George and gave Sally a hug when she handed him a large glass of iced tea. "Glad that my girl brought you to visit again," she said. "What's been goin' on with that haunted statue?"

"More going on than I like," answered Michael, shaking his head, and proceeded to tell them about Stephanie's scary encounter with Aphrodite. He related what he learned about the Greek colony in New Smyrna, Florida. "I'm convinced there is a connection between the story George told us and that colony but I can't prove it. I was hoping that George remembered more details that would help us make that connection."

George puffed on his pipe and shook his head, "I's sorry to say, I don't recollect nothin' new. But what I tol' you is clearer in my mind since we last talked. Folks that tol' the stories wuz sure the statue was found here on the island after a big storm, buried in the sand. And I remember some men who come up from Florida to visit said that they recollect hearin' 'bout a statue in the marsh that was evil, but they didn't know what happen to it."

Michael was disappointed not to learn more from the old man but he felt it was worth the trip just in case. He puzzled over the stories George told and what he had observed himself about Aphrodite. He turned everything over and over in his mind, this way and that way, like a Rubik's Cube, but couldn't get the pieces to fit.

"Let's go inside and see what you brought in that basket," Sally said to Maggie. "We'll get it on the table and then call the men folk. Didn't you say you wanted to look at your Granny's things? What are you lookin' for?"

"I gave my *wanga* bag to Stephanie and I want to see if Granny left any more in her things."

"You know I don't b'lieve in all that stuff your Granny was into, but if it will make you feel better, we'll look and see. There's a couple of boxes in the closet."

The sun was sliding toward the west when Michael and Maggie got on their way back to Savannah. "I know you're disappointed that George didn't have any more information for you," said Maggie. "But, I got two more *wanga* bags and I feel good 'bout that."

"Yes, I am disappointed, but maybe Mrs. Habersham will have some more information from her research at the Georgia Historical Society Library. It would be good to know where the statue came from, but the main thing is we need to come up with a plan how to get rid of it."

Chapter 34

"Good morning, Michael" said Phillip the next morning at the office. "You're here very early. Is there a problem I should know about?"

"No, I just haven't been sleeping well these days, with the senator in Atlanta having surgery. Of course, Stephanie is there with him."

Phillip went to his desk and picked up the day's agenda. "I think you're really stuck on that girl. You need me to give you some advice on how to get more intimate?" He asked, trying to keep a straight face.

"Okay, smart ass," smiled Michael. "My situation is very complicated. But, enough about me. Tell me, how's your love life?"

"Actually, quite good. Peaches helped me fix a place for Mother downstairs in one of the parlors. Mother seems to like her and thanked her for taking care of me when she had her heart attack. Gosh, Michael, Peaches is fantastic. The problem is that I don't think Mother will ever be able to negotiate the long staircase, not even after physical therapy. Peaches suggested that I remodel the downstairs of the carriage house for her, but I don't know how Mother will take that. I don't want her to think I'm pushing her out of her own house."

Peaches bounced into the office, a vision in a clingy red dress and high heels to match. Her bright hair shone like gold under the fluorescent lights. "Morning, guys," she tossed a flirty look at Phillip under long lashes and smirked at Michael. "What's on for today?" She went to her desk, put her purse in the bottom drawer and uncovered her typewriter.

"Well, we have two meetings with prospective brides and mothers and that 300-guest dinner in the ballroom tonight," replied Phillip, reading from the agenda he was holding. "I have you down to talk to the brides and mothers and I'd like Michael to deal with the kitchen staff. He works better with the chef than I do. I'll take care of the paperwork and whatever else comes in." Personal conversation time was over.

During his lunch time, Michael walked to the Georgia Historical Society Library to speak with Mrs. Habersham. He was disappointed that she had no further information for him about the New Smyrna Colony, but enjoyed a short visit with the volunteer librarian while telling her about his visit to St. Augustine.

Back at the office, Michael was glad to find Peaches alone. "How are you and Phillip doing?" he asked. "He told me you and his mother have become friends, and that you are planning to fix up the carriage house for her. So you're planning to move into the big house and take over, are you?"

Peaches eyes flashed green fire. "Listen, I told you before to mind your own business. Have you seen that house? It has four large bedrooms on the second floor and a huge attic with large windows that could be made into a suite. It's perfect for a bed and breakfast and it's just sitting there, while Phillip struggles to pay the utilities and taxes. And, I also told you that I like the guy, maybe even love him, so butt out."

"But the question is this. Would you still like, or maybe love him, if he didn't have that house? You should think about that."

There was no fast comeback from Peaches. She searched Michael's face for a few seconds before answering. "Would you still want that skinny ice princess, Stephanie, without her daddy's money?"

"Absolutely. Boudreau's money doesn't even enter into our relationship. And you can forget that 'ice princess' remark. Stephanie is a wonderful, warm and loving woman."

"Well, I see she's got her hooks into you pretty deep. But, that's your business. As I told you before, stay out of mine. Phillip is happy and I promise he'll get even happier. Isn't that enough?"

After work, Michael couldn't face the house without Stephanie, so he walked down Drayton Street to spend some time with Pinkie. The bar was busy and boisterous with the regular evening crowd. He snagged a stool at the bar and Pinkie poured him a scotch.

"Michael, a police friend of mine is checking the airport for anyone coming in from Las Vegas, but no news yet. I'll call you if we hear anything."

"Thank you, Nono. I was hoping they forgot about me, but I don't think Big Duke will let it slide. What makes it worse is that Stephanie and the senator could be in danger, also. What an idiot I was to tangle with those guys."

Michael wanted to tell his godfather about Stephanie's

experience with Aphrodite, but he didn't think Pinkie would believe him, so he didn't mention it. Instead, he finished his drink, relinquished his barstool, and waved goodbye to Pinkie.

When he arrived at the senator's house, Maggie was in the kitchen, setting the table. "Any word from Stephanie?" he asked.

"Only that they arrived at Catherine's house and the operation is still scheduled for seven in the morning. I've been so worried, I cleaned house all day, though the cleaning women are coming tomorrow. There sure won't be much for them to do."

"I know what you mean. I've been unsettled all day, also. I'm not really hungry right now. Would you mind if I go for a walk before I eat?"

"No, that's okay, but don't go walking in the garden, whatever you do. Let me give you one of the *wanga* bags I got from Mama's yesterday."

"No, I'll be all right." He was still too embarrassed to tell her he was wearing his Yiayias' amulet. I'm just going to walk out to the water and sit on the deck for a while. Are the lights on out there?"

"Are you kidding? I got every light on, inside and outside the house. Don't be too long. I have spaghetti and meatballs. You need to eat somethin'."

Michael walked around the side of the house to the deck and sat down to clear his head. The sky was partially covered with cottony clouds. The moon danced in and out of the wispy clouds as if playing a game of hide and seek, while tree frogs joined in with a chorus. He wanted that cursed statue gone before Stephanie came home. He wondered what would happen if he would smash the statue with a sledge hammer. Aphrodite had never tried to hurt him, but he felt sure the statue would turn on him if he tried to destroy it. After a while, his mind more in a muddle than ever, he walked back to the house.

Chapter 35

G inger's heels echoed down the main hall as she rushed toward the family waiting room of the cancer wing of Emory Hospital. Her chic black suit was wrinkled and her brick-red hair askew from running her hands through it on the way to the hospital. In the waiting room, Stephanie paced the floor and Catherine Woolsey, a handsome woman in her early sixties, sat on a chair, her hands twisting a white lace hankie.

"Oh, Steffie, please forgive me for not being here sooner. I had a class and my professor is an absolute prick and wouldn't let me skip it." She put her arms around her friend and gave her a hug. "Tell me, how is the senator?"

"That's the problem. We don't know anything. He's been in the operating room forever and no one will tell us anything." Stephanie had been holding back tears but when her friend hugged her, the dam broke. "I'm so glad you're here, Ginger. I know I am driving Aunt Catherine to distraction, making her even more upset than she is already."

Ginger walked Stephanie over to one of the small sofas

and sat down with her, scrambling in her large purse for a couple of tissues. "There now, honey, it's okay to cry. It releases the tension."

Turning to Catherine, she said "Hello, Mrs. Woolsey, I'm glad you're here with Stephanie. I know you're both terribly worried, but the senator is a fighter and he'll be up and about in no time. I understand Steffie and the senator will stay with you for a while until he is strong enough to go home. This will give me some time to be with them and maybe help you in some way. As you may know, I am here for a couple of months taking some classes in accounting at Georgia State."

"Thank you for the offer of help and for coming here today," answered Catherine. "We need a cheerful face to perk us up. I'm afraid both Stephanie and I have been doom and gloom. It's just that we love Winston so much, you see. Oh my, here I go crying, too." Catherine pulled out a second lace hanky from her purse.

Close to tears herself, Ginger knew she had to break the tension. "Look here, y'all have to stop crying because I have no more tissues. If you keep this up, we'll have to call someone in to mop the floor." This struck Stephanie funny and she hiccupped and smiled.

Catherine smiled, also. "Bless you, child. I'm so glad you came. Of course my brother is going to be all right. We just need the doctor to come out and tell us so."

As if Catherine's words conjured him up, Dr. Snyder came through the swinging doors of the operating room wearing green scrubs and a smile. His sharp brown eyes beamed first at Stephanie and then at Catherine.

"The senator did very well. We think we got all the

cancer, but he still has a long period of recuperation ahead. We will keep him here for a few days to monitor him. I believe you said he will stay in Atlanta, until he is stronger, which is a good idea."

"Right now, he will be in recovery for a few hours. You can see him when he's taken to his room. I'll talk to you again later and the nurse will have some instructions for you when you visit him."

The three women were so relieved they rushed up to thank Dr. Snyder and shake his hand. Stephanie couldn't help but give him a hug.

"Thank God, this is wonderful news," said Ginger. "However, I bet you girls haven't eaten and it's the middle of the afternoon. I'm taking ya'll out for a late lunch and I don't mean here in the hospital. I know a nice place not too far from here." Ignoring both Stephanie's and Catherine's protests that they 'mustn't leave the hospital', Ginger took Stephanie's arm and gently pulled her down the hall. What could Catherine do but follow?

When they arrived at the restaurant, Stephanie felt that she could actually eat something. It was the first thing she had put in her stomach all day, except for coffee early that morning. From the restaurant, she called Maggie to tell her the good news and asked her to call Michael and tell him she would telephone him that evening.

During lunch, Stephanie and Catherine discussed the schedule for staying with the senator in the hospital. It was decided that Stephanie would stay with him at night and Catherine would spell her in the morning. Ginger wanted to help but Stephanie wouldn't hear of it.

"There is no way you can take a shift since you are working as well as taking classes. If you can drop in whenever you have time or call to see if we need anything, it would be lovely. How fortunate for us that you are here in Atlanta to cheer us up."

"Michael, it's me."

"Oh Steffie. It's so good to hear your voice. How is the senator? How are you?"

"Well, I'm cautiously optimistic. The doctor believes they got all the bad cells, but Daddy has a long recovery and treatment ahead of him. Right now he looks very pale and is hooked up to a lot of equipment. I hate to see him like this but I know they are for his benefit. I'm planning to be right here with him all night."

"Baby, you must be exhausted. Where will you sleep? I wish I could be there with you. Just say the word and I'll drive right over. The hell with my job."

"No, don't come. I know you mean well, but right now I have to concentrate on Daddy. I have a little cot here in his room. I'm sure I'll be fine."

"Okay, but promise me you'll call me if…if you need me. Remember that I love you."

"I remember. I'll call you tomorrow. Goodnight, Michael."

Chapter 36

"Hi boss, it's me, Rocco. Yeah, I'm here in Savannah. Got here this afternoon. God, what a two-bit town this is. The place is dead; no action at all on the main drag. Lots of trees and flowers, if you like that kind of stuff and it's hot as hell. Yeah, yeah, I know what to do. Rough him up a bit, mess up his pretty face, but don't waste him because you don't want no trouble with the cops. I'm staying in a dingy motel near a big bridge so's to keep a low profile. Will call you tomorrow after I find out where he's staying."

Rocco left his room and started a conversation with the elderly man at the motel reception desk. "Say, I'm gonna be in Savannah for a couple of days. Where's a good place to go for some action?"

The room clerk studied the man across the counter. He was about five feet, ten inches tall, stocky build with slicked back brown hair. His eyes were ice blue. He might have been considered nice looking except for his nose that looked like it had been broken more than once. A thug, the room clerk decided and definitely not from the South.

"What kind of action are you looking for?"

"A bar, the kind of place where I can make a bet, meet some girls ya' know. I'd like to get to know some of the locals."

"Well now, there some new places down on River Street, but the locals mostly go to Pinkie's Bar on Drayton Street or to the Sports Center on State Street. I can give you directions and you can walk to either place, easy."

As soon as the visitor left, the clerk dialed a local number, "Hey, Pinkie, it's Fred down at the Southern Motel. The guy you told me to look out for may be staying here. He says he's from Atlanta but he ain't no southerner. Looks like an ex-boxer. Signed in as John Smith. How's that for picking an unusual name. Says he's looking for action so I sent him to your place and the Sports Center. Oh, sure, don't mention it. I owe you."

Pinkie put down the telephone and lit a cigarette from the one hanging out of his mouth before he dialed another number. "Ryan, just got a call from Fred. Said a guy checked in at the motel that looks like the one we're looking for. Stranger said he wanted to meet some locals so Fred sent him here and to the Sports Center. Described him as about 5'10", slicked-back brown hair and full of muscles. No, Fred didn't say if he was carrying."

"What are you going to do? Uh huh, uh huh. Shouldn't I call and warn Michael? I don't want anything to happen to that boy. I'd never be able to face his parents. Okay, okay, I'll wait until you make the contact but don't make me wait too long."

Joe Ryan was an undercover cop, working with the

Savannah police drug squad. He lived on Tybee Island with his wife and two children. If someone saw him driving his kids to school or playing ball with them on the beach, he would see a tall, clean-cut young man. Maybe his hair was a little long and his eyes unusually watchful, but hardly anything that made him stand out.

When on the job in town, he stood with his shoulders hunched; his face and clothes dirty, and almost always appeared half drunk. He wore a filthy black watch cap with part of his hair hanging in his face. Most guys in bars avoided him because he smelled and always tried to borrowed money. Store owners tried to get him to leave but wouldn't call the police because he caused such a ruckus, it would run off the paying customers. They considered him a downtown bum, aggravating but harmless.

Rocco strolled into the Sports Center on State Street and looked around. He had changed into jeans and a t-shirt but his shiny expensive black shoes would have given him away. It looked like a friendly local bar with a high bar on one side and tables along the other wall. A few pool tables were in the middle. Several men were at the bar talking, laughing and drinking. At a corner table, a couple of men were teasing a scruffy-looking guy. He was whining in a loud voice and asking them to buy him a drink.

After a quick look around, Rocco went up to the bar and ordered a beer. "Nice place you got here," he said to the bartender. "Can I make a bet here?"

"Man, don't you know that's against the law in Georgia?" growled the bartender.

"Yes, I heard that, but I also heard that it's possible if you know the right person."

"Sorry, this ain't the right place and you ain't the right person. Now if you want another beer, I can handle that."

"Okay, okay, whatever. Hey, who's that nasty-looking guy over in the corner, the one that's making all the noise?"

" Oh, that's old Crabs. Hey, y'all leave Crabs alone, will ya'?" The bartender called to the guys teasing the scruffy man, "Leave him alone so he'll shut up."

Turning back to the stranger, the bartender continued, "He hangs around the bars in town. They call him Crabs because he was in Matthews Fish Market and a crab grabbed his finger and he almost tore up the whole place before they could get that damn crab to let go. It was hilarious. The guys still tease him about it. When he's not drinking, he won't hurt a fly and he'll do anything for a few bucks."

Rocco looked at Crabs and an idea began to form in his mind. When the guys teasing Crabs left the bar, he took a couple of beers and sat down at the table with him. "Hi, my name's John. I saw those guys picking on you and I wanted to come over and punch them, but, hell, I just got in town and I didn't want to get into trouble. Here, have one on me."

Crabs raised his bowed head and gave the stranger a blank look. "So'kay. I don't mind, they're my friends." He picked up the bottle and chugged it down. "Thanks. Where you from?"

"Oh, here and there. I'm looking for a man here in Savannah. Would you like to help me find him? I can pay real good."

Crabs' blank eyes turned greedy. "Sure, I know eva'body

in town. If he's ever come in a downtown bar, shit, I seen him. What he look like?"

"He's tall, about six one, with dark hair and blue eyes. He wouldn't have a southern accent. Women think he's good-looking, if you like that type," Rocco smirked.

"Don't think I seen him here, but there's bars on River Street. And there's Pinkie's and other bars around town. I'll start checking around. Gimme some money up front."

Knowing he would lose him to drink if he gave him money, Rocco shook his head, "No money until you find the guy. Meet me back here tomorrow morning with what you find out. By the way, where is this Pinkie's?"

After getting directions, Rocco headed for Pinkie's. Since Pinkie's was also mentioned by the guy at the motel, maybe this was the place to go. When he arrived, he was surprised to find Pinkie's a small, dark, unremarkable place. But, it was obviously very popular and full of people who seemed to know each other. There was a small guy behind the bar with a cigarette hanging out of his mouth and one waitress. The customers didn't seem to mind waiting to be served. Rocco stood in line and ordered a whiskey. When a couple vacated a booth, he sat down.

A tired-looking waitress came by to ask if he wanted a refill. Rocco described Michael and asked if she knew him. Julie, a long time waitress at Pinkie's, had been briefed.

"Honey, it stays so busy in here, I ain't got time to notice what these guys look like. They all look like bad news to me." She jerked her head toward the man behind the bar, "You can ask Pinkie, but you gotta come back when it ain't so busy."

Rocco was tired and sleepy after his long trip. He finished his drink and walked back to his motel room. As he started west on Broughton Street and passed Bull Street, a chilly breeze wrapped around him. He shivered and wished he had worn a sweater. The old run-down buildings on either side of the street seemed to lean toward him closing him in. *What a creepy place*, he thought as he picked up his pace and hurried to his motel.

The next morning at eleven Rocco went back to the Sports Center. Crabs was not there. He didn't want to hang around and become conspicuous so he went around the corner and had breakfast. When he came back an hour later, Crabs was at the bar, trying to bum a drink from the bartender. Rocco slid into the stool next to him and turned to the bartender. "Give me and Crabs some coffee."

"Coffee, hell. I want whiskey," whined Crabs. He looked even dirtier and more rumpled than the night before. Probably slept in one of the little parks Rocco had noticed last night.

"Look here, you will stay sober until we find this man I'm looking for. That is if you want to get paid. After that, I don't give a damn if you drink yourself blind. Do you understand me?" He scowled, giving Crabs a look that would loosen the bowels of most men.

"Okay, okay, I gotcha, boss. How 'bout some breakfast then?" he said, looking hopefully at Rocco. "I got some news for you. Somebody down on River Street told me that there's this guy who came to Savannah a while back. Works at the DeSoto Hotel and has some connection with Pinkie Masters. He looks like you described." Crabs gave Rocco a big smile, showing most of his black teeth. "I bet that's worth fifty, ain't it?"

"Good work, pal. Now, don't talk to anybody about this. I may need you again, okay?" He pulled out some bills from his pocket and slid them down the bar. "See ya."

Crabs grabbed the money and called out to the bartender. "Hot damn. Forget the breakfast, Dave. Just bring me the whiskey bottle."

Rocco walked to the main entrance of the DeSoto Hotel, stopped at the steps and took out a pack of cigarettes. He fished around in his pockets pretending to look for a light. "Say buddy," he called to the doorman. "Got a light?"

"Yes suh, here you go." The doorman pulled out a lighter and lit Rocco's cigarette. Having pegged him for a stranger, Jackson asked, "You visitin' in Savannah? Can I help you?"

Rocco masked his annoyance. This is why he liked big cities where you could blend in. His type of job depended on it. "Yes, thanks. I'm supposed to talk to someone who works here at the hotel but I forgot his name. Tall, dark, nice looking young man. A friend of mine asked me to look him up." He shook his head trying to look bewildered.

"Oh, that sounds like Mr. Andrews. He works here in the catering department. He's real nice."

"Thanks, man. Here's something for your trouble." Handing the doorman a five-dollar bill, he ran up the steps into the hotel.

Jackson scratched his head. "That sure was a big tip for just talking. But, why do I care?" he grinned and slipped the money in his pocket.

Later that day, Rocco made a call from a public phone. "Hey, Phil, it's me. Yeah, I found him, working at a hotel here in town. I know what time he gets off from work, but he parks his car in the parking garage below and they're too many people around for me to do him there. I found out he lives out of the city with some guy he made friends with. I got this half-crazy local guy here who will do anything for a drink. I'm gonna get him to go with me to find the place where Andrews is staying. I'll pay him a visit there. Yeah, yeah, I know. Catch you later."

After Crabs told Rocco he had a friend who worked in the hotel kitchen who got him Michael's home address, Rocco rented a car. He told Crabs to meet him later that evening, but to take a bath or he wouldn't let him get in the car with him. When Crabs came back a couple of hours later, he was wearing the same dirty clothes but didn't smell quite as bad.

They got lost a couple of times but finally found the long driveway into the senator's property. Rocco drove in just far enough to see the house clearly, but not close enough to be seen from the house.

"Well, I'll be damned. Look at that setup. Seems like the Greek fell in a pile of shit and came out smelling like a rose."

"Sure looks fancy," said Crabs. "Look, there's someone in the kitchen. Looks like it's a cook. What are we going to do here, boss?"

"Nothing right now. Shut up and let me think." Rocco studied the property carefully, noting the long circular driveway leading to the large house. He saw a path on the left leading to a dock and a garden to the right of the house. There was something white and glowing in the middle of the garden, a statue maybe. Behind the garden stood a smaller structure, probably the carriage house where Michael stayed. There was no other way; he would have to go in on foot.

Rocco backed up the rented car into the woods along a drive used by service trucks. He hid the car behind a copse of trees and told Crabs they would stay in the car and wait.

It wasn't easy, having to listen to Crabs moan and complain. "What are we gonna do here? I want to go back to town and get a drink. Listen man, I'm tired and I gotta pee."

Rocco shoved Crabs out of the car. "Oh, for god's sake, go on out and piss in the woods. What do you need, a marble urinal?"

A few minutes later, he heard a scream and Crabs jumped back in the car, zipping up his filthy pants. "Shit, there's a big snake out there."

By the time Crabs settled down, they heard the sound of an approaching car. A red convertible with Michael at the wheel swung around the curve heading toward the mansion. Rocco smiled to himself. The pigeon was coming home to roost.

"Look Crabs, I have some business there at the house." He jerked his thumb toward the mansion. "You watch for me and when you see me coming back, start up the car and drive out into the road to pick me up. You do know how to drive, don't you?"

"Hell, yeah, I can drive. Whad'ya think? But I'm tired of hanging around here. I want to go back to town. I need a drink," Crabs whined.

Rocco grabbed Crabs by the front of his shirt and pulled him close to his face, his mean eyes gleamed and his mouth twisted. "Don't give me any more shit. Do like I say or I'll leave you here in the woods with the snakes."

Crabs shivered. "Okay, boss, I gotcha'. I'll do anything you say."

Chapter 37

The sun had set and the house was dark except for the light in a downstairs window. *Must be the kitchen where we saw the woman earlier,* thought Rocco. He ran from tree to tree until he reached the garden. Creeping silently on cat feet, he entered lush greenery and summer flowers. The scent was cloyingly sweet. He spotted a pool covered with water lilies. In front of the pool was the statue he had noticed from the drive. Strange, the statue emitted an eerie glow, yet he didn't see any lights directed to it. Maybe it was the full moon which had now begun its journey through the dark sky. His first thought was to hide behind the statue, but something made him decide not to. He found a large gardenia bush covered with white blossoms, took his sap out of his pocket and crouched low.

After Rocco left, Crabs waited a few minutes before leaving the car. Once outside, he straightened his shoulders, stretched his back, and reached under his tattered sweater for the gun he had hidden at the small of his back. He quietly followed Rocco until he reached the end of the trees and hid where he had a good view of the garden. When he heard nothing but normal night noises, he crept to the garden wall and stopped there.

Upstairs in the carriage house apartment, Michael received a phone call from Pinkie. He took off his work clothes and changed into jeans and a t-shirt. He looked out the window to check out the garden. He didn't see anything suspicious except that goddamn Aphrodite was glowing again. He picked up his telephone and dialed the main house number.

"Maggie, listen, I got a call from Pinkie. Looks like a man has come to Savannah looking for me but I don't know if he will come here or approach me at work."

"Oh Lordy, lordy, should we call the police?" Maggie grabbed her *wanga* bag.

"No, Maggie, don't be frightened. Pinkie said there's an undercover cop with him and he won't let him hurt anyone. We're just to go on like usual and let the policeman take care of it. I know, I'm nervous, too. Why don't we forget dinner? Lock up the house, turn off the lights, and go upstairs. Take the pistol that's in the senator's desk upstairs with you."

"No, I ain't gonna touch that gun. I'd probably just shoot myself. I'd feel better if you was here. Please come on over. Your dinner's already on the table."

"Okay, but look out the kitchen window. If you see anyone but me walking down the garden path, then, you call the police."

Michael opened the door of the carriage house and looked out. The moon sent shimmering light across the garden. Nothing moved. The absence of sound screamed in his ears. He closed the door quietly and started down the path toward the kitchen door when a shrub at the side of the path erupted and a searing pain at the back of his head crumbled him to the ground. Immediately, someone was on top of him raining blows at his face and head. Michael was big and strong and had defended himself admirably in his younger days on school playgrounds and Chicago streets, but he was no match for Rocco.

Rocco continued pummeling his face and head. When Michael tried to get his hands around his assailant's neck, he could feel blood running from his nose into the back of his throat. He pushed up with his legs and the two of them began to roll over and over toward the statue of Aphrodite until they bumped into the base. Michael tried with all his might to hold on to consciousness, and was barely aware of someone else grabbing the collar of his assailant and trying to pull him off. Rocco was so engrossed in inflicting pain, he paid no attention to the other person who joined the fight, but continued to aim blows on Michael's head.

Ryan could see that Michael was badly hurt so he shouted, "Stop! Police!" and fired his revolver into the air.

At the sound of gunfire, Rocco released Michael and turned to see Crabs crouched in a shooting stance, pointing a pistol at him. He hardly had time to figure out what had happened when the head of Aphrodite crashed down and knocked him to the ground. The statue seemed to glow brighter for an instant and then it exploded into pieces.

Ryan grabbed the semi-conscious Michael under the arms and dragged him away from the raining chunks of marble and went back for Rocco. But it was too late. Rocco was dead, buried under a pile of marble pieces. Ryan scratched his head. *What the hell happened*, he wondered.

At the kitchen window, Maggie, her eyes wide with

horror, was the lone observer. One hand was holding the telephone and the other was over her mouth to keep from screaming. Minutes later, a patrol car and an ambulance charged down the drive and screeched to a stop. Maggie had called 911.

Michael was taken to the hospital to have his broken nose set and to be checked for possible concussion. After the ambulance left, Ryan went into the house and spoke to Maggie. She was sitting at the kitchen table with her head in her hands.

"Please tell me that Michael is okay. Stephanie can't take losing another person she loves." She looked up anxiously. "I guess you're the policeman Michael told me about."

"Yes, I'm Detective Joe Ryan and a friend of Pinkie's. Michael's pretty messed up but not seriously hurt. The paramedics said he'll be okay. I've had my eye on that guy from Vegas ever since he hit town. Now, can you tell me what you saw through the window? Please do that for me because I'm a little confused as to what happened."

"Okay, but first let me get a cup of coffee. I'm still a little shaky"

"Here, don't get up. Let me get the coffee for you and I'll get one for myself. Are these cups here on the drain board okay to use?" He brought two cups of coffee to the table and sat down. "Now, take your time, but tell me exactly what you witnessed."

Maggie took a sip of coffee. She looked toward the window and shivered. "I was watching out the window for Michael to cross the garden and come in the back door. I saw a man jump out of a bush and hit Michael on the head with something he was holding in his hand. Michael fell down and this guy jumped him. I just froze up. Then I remember Michael told me to call 911 if anything happen." She took a couple of long breaths and sipped some more coffee. "Then, the two of them was fighting and rolling toward that statue. And then, somebody else was there." She pointed at Ryan. "That musta been you, right?" Ryan nodded.

"You was holding a gun and you yelled something and then you shot that devil statue."

"What?" I didn't shoot the statue. I shot in the air to stop Rocco from doing any more damage to Pinkie's godson."

"Well, yes you did. I saw the bullet go into the statue's neck and then the whole head fell off and knocked the bad man down. That evil statue has been shiny pink for the last couple of days. But, after the head fell off, it got even pinker and then it just blew up and that sorry man was covered up with all the pieces. I think the statue killed him."

Ryan shook his head, "I hope the captain believes this story. For sure, the whole squad will be laughing at me for shooting a statue in the line of duty. Someone else will probably be out in the morning to take down your statement. Are you sure this is what happened?"

"Yes suh, it happened exactly like I told you."

The next morning, Michael came home with a bandaged nose, two black eyes, a cut lip, plus a horrific headache. "Good Lawd, you look terrible." Maggie threw up both hands when he walked into the kitchen. "Steffie's gonna be upset when she sees you. She called early this morning to say the senator wants to come home, so they're coming next week."

Moving rather stiffly, Michael sat down at the table. "Yes, she probably will, and I also have bruises that don't show. I'm glad they're coming home but we have work to do before they get here."

"What you mean, we? What kind of work?"

"We can't leave that rubble out there in the garden. When the police let us, we have to get rid of the pieces of the statue and get a replacement."

"Not me. I ain't touching any part of that evil thing."

"I wouldn't ask you to do that. I want you to call José to help me load it into his truck and take it to a dump someplace. What do you think about a nice fountain to take its place? We can say the statue fell over and broke and couldn't be fixed. The senator mentioned once that the base was unsteady. I guess I'll have to say my bruises are from an accident at work."

Maggie called José and he came the next morning. Michael and the gardener loaded the marble pieces into heavy plastic bags and took them to a dumping area in a neighboring county, sixty miles from Savannah. Michael didn't want a single piece of Aphrodite left anywhere near the senator's house. When placing the pieces in the garbage bags, he could feel the warmth of the marble even through heavy garden gloves. *Shouldn't the marble be cold? It must be my imagination*, he decided.

On the way to the dump, he thought about the gold ring he had put on Aphrodite's finger. Even if he had seen it in the rubble, he wouldn't have touched it.

Chapter 38

A week later, Stephanie and her father drove back to Savannah. The senator was happy to be home but tired after the drive and went straight to bed for a nap. He didn't notice the statue of Aphrodite was missing or the new fountain in the garden.

"What happened to your face, boy?" he asked when Michael pushed the wheelchair into his room.

"Just a little accident at work," he replied. "It's nothing. The swelling will go down soon."

The Senator took another look at Michael's face as the younger man helped him into bed. "Don't be too sure. That bump on your nose may not completely go away. Hope Steffie won't mind your not having a perfect Grecian nose anymore." He turned on his side and was asleep before Michael could remove his shoes.

Michael didn't realize how prophetic the senator's words were. He would always have a little bump on his nose, as a remembrance of his encounter with Aphrodite.

Once the senator was taken care of and Maggie went into the kitchen to start dinner, Michael put his arms around Stephanie and held her close. Stephanie snuggled into his warm arms, aware that this was where she belonged. Being away from him made her realize how much she loved him. Michael ran his hands down her body to her hips and pulled her tight, letting her feel his arousal. "Baby, you have no idea how much I've missed you. I need to be close to you. Your room or mine?"

Stephanie pulled back and looked at Michael's face. "I need you, too, but are you going to tell me what happened to your nose? Maybe this is good," she teased. "Now, maybe you won't be prettier than me."

"Are you kidding me? You're the most beautiful woman in the whole world. Let's go upstairs to my apartment and let me show you that I worship every single part of you."

Stephanie took his hand, and as they went out the front door, she called back, "Maggie, we'll be upstairs in the carriage house if the Daddy needs anything."

Maggie smiled. "You be careful, Steffie."

When they entered the garden, Stephanie stopped dead when she saw the fountain of Cupid, where Aphrodite once stood. "Michael, how did you manage to get rid of the statue? You said you were afraid to touch it. This has something to do with your injuries, hasn't it? You have to tell me what happened."

"I will, I promise, but right now, I want you naked and under me in my bed. It's been too long. I've been crazy to hold you." He led her up the stairs and into his apartment and closed the door. He had such a wild look in his eyes Stephanie expected he would rip off her clothes and she hoped he would. She could hardly wait to have that gorgeous hard body wrapped around her. She wanted him inside of her, right now.

Instead, Michael took her hand and led her slowly to the bed and sat down next to her. He took her in his arms and kissed her tenderly, then deepened the kiss. His mouth moved to her eyes, her cheeks, her brow and her neck. He kissed the tender place behind her ears. Each time his lips touched her, hot liquid shot to her center.

Michael slowly unbuttoned her blouse. He kissed her collarbone and the soft plump flesh above her bra. Stephanie raised her hands to unhook her bra, but Michael's hand stayed hers. He pulled down the straps and her breasts were revealed, the rose colored nipples distended. He ran his finger over one of her nipples an it hardened instantly. Stephanie heard a moan and wondered if it came from her.

He took the tight nipple into his mouth and suckled it. Stephanie leaned back on the bed and moaned again, as he paid the same attention to the other breast. Michael slowly removed Stephanie's clothes, one item at the time, kissing the area he uncovered each time. When he slid off her panties and kissed her hot, throbbing center, Stephanie grabbed the mattress and raised her hips. He quickly climbed out of his jeans and shirt and buried himself inside her in one swift thrust.

Much later as they lay in each other's arms, Michael nibbled on Stephanie's ear, "I love you so much. I don't want to be away from you ever again."

"I love you, too and I missed you so much."

"Steffie, let's not wait to get married. I want us to be together like this every day."

Stephanie put her head on his shoulder and ran her fingers

through the soft, dark hair on his chest and whispered, "I've been thinking the same thing."

"I know I said I wanted to wait until I could prove I could take care of you, but because of that damned statue, I realized that anything can happen. Life is too short. Would you mind not having a big wedding?"

"Michael, with Daddy having all those treatments ahead of him, I wouldn't have time to plan a big wedding. As long as you, Daddy, Maggie and Ginger are there, I'll be happy. Of course, Pinkie, too. What about your parents? Will they come?"

"I've been putting off calling Mom and Dad until I talked with you. I think they will come."

After leaning over and kissing the bump on his nose, Stephanie wrapped the sheet around her and plumped the pillows. "Okay, now that the wedding is settled, I want to hear what happened to Aphrodite."

Michael sat up and put his arms around Stephanie. "Okay, but don't get upset because there is nothing to fear any more. The statue is gone and it will never hurt you or anyone else ever again." Then, he told her the whole story.

The next day, Michael went to Pinkie's Bar to see his godfather. "Nono, you saved my life. I've thanked you before, but I want to thank you again. And, Lt. Ryan, too."

Pinkie's face beamed as Michael walked around the bar and gave him a big hug. "You don't have to thank me. It's my responsibility as your godfather to look after you, but I never expected to go to such extremes, like having to save your life. Don't worry about Ryan, either. He's a good friend and was glad to help. Now, can I call your parents and ask them to come down? I'm anxious to see Anna and Gus. It's been a while since they visited Savannah."

"You don't have to. I've already called and they'll be down soon. I'll let you know when their travel plans are complete. Now, here's even bigger news. Stephanie and I are going to get married while my parents are here."

Pinkie opened his mouth in surprise, which meant he had to remove his cigarette—a rare happening indeed.

Chapter 39

Two weeks later…

The reunion at the airport between Michael and his parents was tearful, yet joyful, with lots of hugs and kisses. Anna saw the difference in her son right away, not only in his mature appearance but in the confidence in his voice. She was so grateful to have him in her arms in one piece. In the car, on the way to the senator's house, Michael talked, explaining why he had come to Savannah, his meeting with the senator in Pinkie's bar, and his subsequent relationship with Stephanie.

"Mom and Dad, I can't wait for you to meet Stephanie. She is the most wonderful girl in the world. She is sweet and caring, as well as smart and beautiful. I am so lucky that she loves me and has agreed to marry me. I know you'll love her, too."

The scene at the Boudreau mansion was just as emotional, with more hugging and kissing and everyone talking at once. Anna and Gus were impressed with the senator's southern charm. Pale but happy, he insisted that Michael's parents stay at the house instead of going to a hotel. Anna was satisfied to see that Stephanie seemed to love her son as much as he loved Stephanie. Maggie, who was introduced to Michael's parents as the only mother Stephanie remembered, had cooked a fabulous dinner, and at Stephanie's insistence, she sat with the family at the dinner table.

After dinner, Boudreau went to his room to rest and Gus asked Michael to drive him back to town to visit with Pinkie. "Sure, Dad, I'll be glad to take you. How about you, Mom? Would you like to come, too?"

Anna took Maggie's hand and put her arm around Stephanie, "No, I think I'll stay here to unpack and get acquainted with my new family. I think we women should talk a little about the wedding. Give Pinkie my love and tell him I'll see him tomorrow."

After Michael and Gus left, the women sat in the kitchen to enjoy another cup of coffee. "Stephanie, have you thought about where you want to have the wedding?" asked Anna.

"Not really, I suppose Michael and I haven't had time to talk about it. Daddy used to take me to Sunday school at the Episcopal Church, but then I want away to school. Since I've been back, well…"

Anna gave Stephanie her most persuasive smile, and touched the gold cross that hung around her neck. "I have a wonderful idea, but it will have to be agreeable to both you and the senator."

Gus was surprised when Michael drove straight to River Street instead of going to Pinkie's Bar. "What are we doing here?" he asked. "If I remember correctly, Pinkie's Bar is on Drayton."

Michael parked the car and turned to his father, "Dad, I want you to see the changes that have been made here on River Street. Rousakis Plaza, named for Mayor John Rousakis, is almost finished. Notice how many more specialty shops and places to eat have opened. In a few years, this street will be the hub of the tourist area in Savannah."

"Let's get out of the car. I want to show you something." Michael led the way down the cobbled street, paved with stones originally used as ballast on ships that crossed the Atlantic Ocean hundreds of years ago. He stopped in front of a boarded-up building facing the Savannah River. "I wanted you to see this because I think it would be a great site for a Greek restaurant."

Gus was confused. "Son, I thought you knew I retired. Your mother wants us to travel. I'm not looking to open another business."

"No, Dad. I want to open a restaurant—for me. But I can't do it without your help. I've learned a little about food from working with the hotel food staff and I remember some things about running a restaurant from you, maybe through osmosis." He grinned. "I know I didn't help you very much, but some of the things you said did stick. However, there is so much I don't know that need you to teach me."

"I want to have something tangible to offer Stephanie. It's a matter of pride." Michael lowered his head for a minute and then looked up at his father with a twinkle in his eyes. "Maybe my Greek restaurant genes have finally surfaced."

Gus was stunned. His heart leaped inside his chest and he put his hand on it as if he feared it would jump out of his body. He had stopped hoping that his younger son would follow in his footsteps since Michael had made that clear, years ago. He didn't know whether to shout, kiss Michael or break out in tears.

He took a few seconds to control his emotions and answered, "Of course, my son. I'll be glad to help you any way I can."

Then he shouted, "Thank God!" and grabbed Michael to kiss him on both cheeks. They stood there, clasped in each other's arms for a couple of minutes as people walked warily around them, shaking their heads.

"Tourists," they mumbled. "Savannah's going to hell in a hand basket"

Chapter 40

It was no surprise that Stephanie made a stunning bride. She wore a tea-length dress of white silk with a modest round neck and long sleeves. Her dark hair was a long smooth waterfall topped by a small crown of pearls and diamonds. Additional diamonds winked at her ears and throat. In her hands, she carried bouquet of pink and white roses. But it was her lovely face, glowing with happiness that was her most beautiful accessory.

There was no procession. Michael, resplendent in a dark suit and snow white shirt, stood with Stephanie on the *solea* facing the altar. His eyes never left his bride. Serving as best man was Michael's brother, Deno. The local priest, Father Franko, dressed in gold and white robes, officiated.

The ceremony took place at St. Paul's Greek Orthodox Church on Bull Street, a Savannah historic building, formerly a concert hall, built in 1898 by the Lawton family. The Greek community purchased the property in 1941 and remodeled it to serve as a Greek Orthodox Church.

Sitting at the front pew on the bride's side of the church were Boudreau, Maggie, Ginger, and Aunt Catherine. On the groom's side, were Anna and Gus, Pinkie, Phillip, and

Peaches. During the ceremony, Maggie and the senator shed a few tears, but Anna and Gus smiled with great happiness. Anna was sure that the icons of the Holy Family and the Saints, decorating the walls of the church, were also smiling.

Afterwards, the new couple shared a lovely brunch with their guests at the Boudreau mansion. The brunch was sponsored by the groom's parents and catered by the Desoto Hotel. The senator couldn't understand why both Stephanie and Michael were adamant about not having the wedding brunch out in the garden.

Chapter 41

O n a bright summer morning, Stephanie parked her new SUV on River Street and slid slowly out onto the cobbled stone street. Although the sky was cerulean blue with only a small scattering of cottony clouds, the street was still wet from an early morning shower. There was no one else in view, since the stores had not yet opened. She stepped up on the sidewalk, one hand protectively over her stomach in which slept their child. As she carefully walked toward the corner where construction was in progress, Michael ran out to meet her.

"Good God, Steffie, you shouldn't have come alone. I thought Maggie was coming with you. You know how dangerous it is to walk on these cobbled streets, especially now that you're pregnant." He put one arm around her shoulders and caressed her distended stomach with his other hand.

"I'm fine," she laughed. "You've got to stop worrying about me and the baby or you'll be in the hospital before I have to go." She raised her face for a kiss. "How's the construction of the Olympic Grill coming along?"

"It's coming, but not fast enough to suit me. Dad says not to be anxious because it's more important that the work be done correctly, not just fast. The folks are coming down next month, Mom to coo over the baby that should be here by then, and Dad to check out the work on the restaurant."

Michael put both arms around Stephanie, careful not to hold her too tight. He looked down at the woman he loved. "When you met me a year and a half ago, did you ever think we would be together like this?"

"Oh, I don't know," she returned his look, eyes shining with love. "When I first met you in Daddy's study, you speared me with those sexy turquoise eyes. Then, soon after that, you gave me that killer kiss the night we met on the front portico. I think I was already hooked; I just didn't know it. Now, take me inside and show me what's been done since I was here last."

Epilogue

I t was midnight on a chilly October night. Rain clouds in a charcoal sky blocked the stars and the moon. In the caretaker's shed at a garbage dump in Effingham County, Rufus dozed in an old BARCO lounger he had salvaged from a stack of broken furniture. The chair was stuck in one position and some of the stuffing had leaked out, but he didn't care. He brought one of Belle's old comforters to cover it, so it suited him just fine.

Sleeping at Rufus' feet was Killer, his pit bull. Killer was ten years old and had lost most of his teeth, but he looked mean enough to scare the teenagers that climbed over the fence once in a while to see what they could steal. Old Rufus was scary looking enough himself with his baggy clothes and long white beard and mustache.

Rufus liked working at night. Ever since Belle, his wife of fifty years passed, he couldn't sleep in their bed. They had no children and he was never close to the rest of his family. Yup, spending the night with old Killer in the caretaker's shed was okay with him. Besides, there was a small fridge there with cold drinks and sandwiches if he got hungry, and a stove if the weather turned cold. Rufus had a military background so he knew how to use a gun, but he only carried a BB gun on his rounds, just to scare trespassers. He might shoot at a rat once in a while just for fun.

Suddenly, Killer raised his huge head, perked up his scarred ears and gave a low growl. Rufus opened his eyes.

"What is it, boy? Hear sumpin? Prob'ly them damn kids."

Killer growled again and looked toward the door. Rufus got out of the chair and hitched up his britches. After grabbing the BB gun and a flashlight, he followed Killer outside.

The air had a sticky feel to it. Smells of damp earth and ripe garbage drifted on the night breeze. Killer walked half way around the dump before he stopped in front of a pile of garbage and discarded items that Rufus was sure had been there at least a year. From time to time, more junk was dumped on top until the pile was almost eight feet tall.

Killer stared at the pile of junk and the hair behind his head stood straight up as he growled low in his throat. Rufus ran the flashlight up and down, right and left, but didn't see anything.

"Don't see nothin' here, boy. What's got you spooked?"

Just as Rufus started to turn away, the beam of light hit something white, something smooth and shiny. It was a woman's hand!

"Dear God, somebody buried a body under all that trash. We gotta call the cops. Good boy, Killer. You still got what it takes." He leaned down to pat Killer on the head, bringing his eyes closer to the hand.

"Wait, this ain't no human hand. It looks like marble.

Must be a broke statue somebody threw out. Hey, what's that on one of them fingers? A gold ring? Maybe we oughta take that." As Rufus reached out to slip the ring from the marble finger, Killer began to howl.

Later, when Rufus tried to remember exactly what happened next, he was confused. As he reached for the ring, the hand seemed to slide back under the pile of garbage. At the same time, the ground shook and the top of the pile came down so that both Rufus and Killer had to jump back to keep from being hit by falling debris.

Killer put his tail between his legs and slunk back toward the shed. Rufus considered digging in the junk to find the gold ring, but decided Killer knew best.

Rufus told the story of the marble hand with the gold ring many times, but nobody ever believed it.

About the Author

Bess Turner Chappas was born in Greece, but came to Savannah by way of Greenville, SC. Although she has traveled to many places around the world, she believes Savannah is the best possible place to live. After a career as teacher and media specialist with the Savannah/Chatham County School System, she wrote a column for Coastal Senior magazine for more than a decade. Chappas has published two children's books, based on her early life in Athens, Greece, Kiki and the Red Shoes *and* Kiki and the Statue of Liberty. *Currently, she is working on a memoir about her mother, a strong and interesting woman who lived to age ninety-eight.*

CPSIA information can be obtained at www.ICGtesting.com
Printed in the USA
LVOW10s1749290315

432490LV00001B/1/P